T0198589

Books by Robert E. Gribbin

NON-FICTION:
In the Aftermath of Genocide – the U.S. Role in Rwanda

FICTION:
State of Decay – An Oubangui Chronicle
Murder in Mombasa

BLOG:
www.rwandakenya.blogspot.com

The Last RHINO

ROBERT GRIBBIN

THE LAST RHINO

iUniverse books may be ordered through booksellers or by contacting:

iUniverse
1663 Liberty Drive
Bloomington, IN 47403
www.iuniverse.com
1-800-Authors (1-800-288-4677)

Because of the dynamic nature of the Internet, any web addresses or links contained in this book may have changed since publication and may no longer be valid. The views expressed in this work are solely those of the author and do not necessarily reflect the views of the publisher, and the publisher hereby disclaims any responsibility for them.

Any people depicted in stock imagery provided by Getty Images are models, and such images are being used for illustrative purposes only. Certain stock imagery © Getty Images.

ISBN: 978-1-5320-9966-3 (sc)
ISBN: 978-1-5320-9967-0 (e)

Print information available on the last page.

iUniverse rev. date: 04/29/2020

This book is dedicated to the last rhinos, innocent victims of human greed. Let us hope and work to ensure that they may yet survive!

The Last Rhino

"The survival of our wildlife is a matter of grave concern to all of us in Africa. These wild creatures and the wild places they inhabit are not only important as a source of wonder and inspiration but are an integral part of our natural resources and of our future livelihood and wellbeing." Julius Nyerere, The Arusha Declaration, 1961

"I had seen a herd of elephants traveling through dense native forest…pacing along as if they had an appointment at the end of the world." Isak Dinesen

"Everything has an end." Masai saying

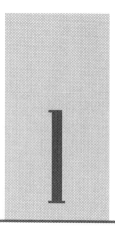

The great fiery orb of the sun inched downward to touch the distant horizon. It hung there for a moment splashing orange onto the surrounding sea, then slowly sank beyond the curvature of the planet. Philippe watched carefully in those last seconds for the green flash, but it did not come. 'Too bad,' Philippe thought to himself, 'sometimes it happens - often it doesn't. But it might have been my last chance for a while.' He settled back comfortably on the cushion in the cockpit and sipped his gin tonic. He gazed fondly at his ship, the *Miss Jill*, a forty-six-foot ketch rigged Morgan sailboat, his home and business for the past five years. She was a taut blue-water ship. With berths for seven, she was perfect for the Caribbean charter business. Philippe had labored on her, keeping her spit polished clean and mechanically sound. "I'm gonna miss you old girl," he muttered under his breath.

The waves lapped quietly against the gunwales and the breeze blew gently. St Pierre, Martinique was a wonderful place to be. It had been Philippe's refuge. His place to think, ponder and heal. He had gotten his second wind there after calamitous events and an airplane crash in Africa had left him half dead and doubting whether life was worth it. Upon first arriving in Martinique he had bounced around, drank too much, but finally cleared his head and buckled down. He crewed for several months on various charters while sorting out his options, then to his delight found a well-kept Morgan on a for sale list in neighboring Antigua. He flew over to St. John's, checked her out and arranged the purchase. After a refit in St. Pierre, Philippe christened his boat *Miss Jill*, named after a lost love, and went into the sailboat charter business himself.

Philippe listed with a local broker and got enough clients to pay expenses. He preferred parties of four, who fit nicely into the two cabins. Over the years he acquired a number of return clients, mostly French or Americans, with whom he built solid friendships. They inevitably asked about his background. Even though he had nothing to hide, Philippe was reticent to reveal much of his life story. Born and raised in France, with a few years of university under his belt he set out to see the world. He bummed around Asia but found Africa entrancing. Taught hunting by his grandfather in the Pyrenees mountains, Philippe apprenticed himself to a professional hunter in Central Africa. He found his calling in the bush. He loved the solitude, the dry heat, the smells and the thrill of the chase. After several years he bought out his mentor and kept the safari operation running smoothly. Philippe was deliberately vague about quitting the hunting business only saying that corruption and politics made it impossible to continue. A vagabond again he pitched up in Martinique and thought he'd try sailing. So here he was. This was usually enough to satisfy curiosity.

Keeping hunting clients happy was part of the earlier job, a skill that easily transferred to sailing clients. Good food, good stories and good sailing were most important. Equally key was knowing when to back away and let the clients enjoy themselves alone. When a first mate was needed Philippe took along Adam Bonmarche, a local boatman, jack-of-all-trades, competent sailor and excellent company. Adam was also a skilled fisherman whose knowledge of local waters was a decided plus when there was a fishing client aboard. Philippe had tried out several cooks over the years. The best was an Australian girl named Sheila. A striking blonde she was a brash Australian to the core, and let Phillipe know in no uncertain terms that she'd heard all the Sheila jokes and innuendos before and would not tolerate any from him. "Understood," he replied. They had a fling together, a shipboard romance that lasted for several months, but the twenty-year age gap ended up being too much. They parted amicably. That had been almost a year ago.

Sheila told him before they split. "Philippe, you are bored here and getting boring. You need something new, something challenging, perhaps a sail around the world, a quest for pirate treasure, or even a passion for big fish, but now you are just sliding slowly into old age."

Philippe was stung by her rebuke. "I am only fifty-one," he retorted.

"Yeah, but you are acting older. Get some energy!"

Afterwards, he reflected on her criticism. She made a good point. He was getting bored. The cruising life was quite comfortable, but not very challenging. Even hurricanes were predictable enough so as to be avoided... and nothing was really trying to kill you. She was right, for years he had not felt the adrenaline rush that arose from stalking a wounded bull cape buffalo in dense bush.

Philippe remembered that conversation with Sheila. She had indeed starting him thinking. About then he read the monthly email magazine from the London based Elephant Conservation Project (ECP). That organization remained about his only contact with Africa. It was also his last link to Jill, for whom the boat was named. Philippe was a regular contributor to the organization. He knew that big game, elephants and rhinos especially, were under great pressure from habitat loss and poaching. He hardly ever saw rhino during his fifteen years of hunting but had regularly combatted elephant poaching. So the monthly reminder that the crisis continued - and that additional funding was sorely needed - was not unexpected. However, the last issue also contained a help wanted ad. The Project anticipated posting a game expert to Garamba Park in the Democratic Republic of Congo to census the elephant population and to help the DRC park authorities devise better methods for protecting them. It solicited interest.

Philippe mulled over the possibility, then decided that he was interested. He truly wanted to get back to the bush. Going as a conservationist was completely acceptable. His hunting days had been good, great even from time to time, but that phase of life was over. It was time to move on from hunting and move on also from the sailing business. He carefully wrote up a resume that highlighted his African experience, his firsthand knowledge of elephants, how they lived and what they did. With some trepidation that he might not be what they wanted, he posted his application to London. Philippe did not have to wait long. He got an email a week later from Stuart McKinney, director of the ECP. McKinney said that Philippe appeared to fit their criteria. Could they Skype? He gave a contact and a time.

I n London at Elephant Conservation Project headquarters Stuart finished the call and sat thinking. He asked his deputy Susan to come in and reviewed his conversation with Philippe with her.

"He sounds just right," Stuart advised. "So I have tentatively offered the job and asked him to come to London next week. He agreed and will be here."

"Great," Susan replied. "So, what's the issue?"

"Well, he may be too much a hunter," he paused thoughtfully, "and he may have too much of an independent streak. We don't want things mucked up out there. Other contracts may flow pending the success of this one."

She chortled, "You worry too much. For God's sake, it is the Democratic Republic of the Congo we're talking about. How much more mucked up could it be?"

"Yeah, but I am especially concerned about the infiltration of Madame Ching's operation. That is not really part of the Garamba project, but should I tell or involve Philippe in it?"

"Wait and take his measure in person. He will certainly have to know but mixing him in – at least initially - might not be a good idea."

S he raised her trunk again and sniffed the air. Something was not quite right. The scents of dust and acacia blossoms were normal, but there was something un-natural. She turned with ears flapping and smelled again. She harumped a danger signal to her family. They moved smartly off into the brush. The matriarch faced the unknown. In her anxiety she pawed the ground and shook her massive head from side to side. Her big feet pushed up clouds of dust. In an instant she saw, heard and smelled the source of danger. Trumpeting loudly, she charged, bashing through the acacia grove towards the blurs of blue. All her instincts required that she do her duty. She must protect her family. As she had done many times before, she would confront the danger - lions, buffalo or perhaps a stray rhino - and chase it away. Her size, the awesome spectacle of an irritated two-ton beast closing rapidly, usually worked. But not this time.

Shots rang out. She was met with a burst of automatic weapon fire. The noise and the smoke were terrifying. She stumbled and fell but was shot yet again, this time from closer range. Bullets fired directly into her brain. Her body convulsed and shuttered. She was dead.

Cries of triumph rose around the dead elephant as the shooters emerged from the trees. Soon two of them manned axes to chop away the matriarch's tusks. They were not the great heavy tusks of a mature bull, but each would weigh about forty pounds - a quite respectable haul for the poachers. They took nothing but the tusks, leaving the carcass to scavengers. The butchers did their work quickly. They wanted to be safely gone before vultures signaled the murder.

The fleeing herd of terrified elephants ran for miles before slowing. They waited impatiently for their boss lady who never came. The transition to new leadership was befuddling, but someone had to take charge. One of the older cows sensed it was now her job. She led the group to water.

ROBERT GRIBBIN

Philippe had some housekeeping to tend to before leaving Martinique. He arranged to lease *Miss Jill* to Adam, his sometime first mate, for a ridiculously meager sum provided that Adam took good care of the vessel. Adam was delighted and promised to keep her shipshape. Philippe closed out his apartment, said a few goodbyes. Shelia was not around so he left a note saying he was following her advice to try something new. Given his private nature, Phillipe preferred to slip out of town without fanfare. He took the evening flight to Paris, spent a few days there then on to London.

Headquarters for the Elephant Conservation Project was just off Piccadilly Circus. The office was one flight up. A cheery receptionist introduced herself as Madge and without a blink said, "you must be Philippe Darman." He nodded affirmation. Before walking him down a corridor to see Stuart and Susan, she confided that everyone was dying to meet him.

Stuart McKinney, a bespectacled rusty haired Scotsman who sported a short beard, extended his hand in greeting. He introduced Susan, his deputy, a long-legged English woman with a very proper accent. Stuart said that the two of them had been running the ECP for about five years. Over that time contributions had steadily increased as had the ECP's ability to attract big donor money. Although still a small outfit compared to conservation organizations with a global reach, ECP had registered successes in its chosen niche – the protection of elephants. They were increasingly focused on elephants in the Congo basin. So that is how the effort for safeguarding the elephant population in Garamba Park came about.

The two briefed Phillipe in greater detail about the Garamba Project. Garamba Park was one of the last great refuges for elephants. Larger than Belgium, located in northeastern Congo, it abutted South Sudan. Therein was the problem. That area of the Congo itself and especially the neighboring parcels of South Sudan and nearby Central African Republic were ungoverned territory, almost completely neglected by their far distant capitals. With little government presence, lawlessness abided and poaching flourished. The wildlife of Garamba was under enormous pressure. Consequently, global conservation organizations had banded together to convince the government of Congo that something had to be done to protect its animal heritage. The government had earlier employed Parks South Africa to manage Garamba, but within months, citing "non-performance," the powers that be cancelled the contract.

"Non-payment of bribes," Stuart scoffed.

NGOs were now ready to step in. The government was on board with the census project and guard training that the Elephant Conservation Project was preparing to do. The agreement was duly signed by the Minister for Wildlife and Tourism, so Philippe would not be tasked to negotiate.

"Thank God for that," Philippe exclaimed.

"Indeed," Stuart retorted. "It wasn't a difficult sell. The minister was on board immediately with the idea, especially with resources coming from abroad. But the details were dicey. Divvying up how much went to the ministry and how much to the project directly was a delicate negotiation, but that is all worked out now."

Philippe replied, "I hope those are not famous last words."

"Me too," Stuart agreed.

Looking again at Philippe's resume, Stuart asked, "can you tell me more about your time in the Central African Republic?"

"Of course," Philippe replied. "I initially apprenticed to a professional hunter there, then inherited his business and concessions when he retired. I usually had a half dozen clients a season who were interested in trophy animals. They were able to shoot what was on their license and occasionally that meant an elephant. However, the trophies of choice in CAR were a derby eland, the antelope with the largest rack of horns, and a huge bull cape buffalo. As was true with most professional hunters, I was a quasi-game warden, my outfit's presence in my hunting concessions helped to keep poachers out. In doing that sort of patrolling, I learned how they operate. Most common were locals who sought meat for the pot and did so with snares or bows and arrows targeting small antelope. We had some Chadian raiders who came on horseback who sought only to kill giraffe, just to cut off their tails as trophies. Finally, we did have some ivory hunters – mostly Sudanese – who sought out the big tuskers. Fortunately, my concessions were not good elephant country, even so I had to confront Sudanese armed groups several times. On those occasions, the arrival of our vehicles was enough to move them along. I and other professionals made it a practice to keep each other as well as CAR officials aware of elephant poachers in the area. Sadly, the government's ability to respond was minimal.

"As a hunter, I initially enjoyed the sport but as time went by, I came to appreciate more deeply the balance of nature in the bush. Every creature has its niche and the whole is greater than the sum of its parts. Elephants are crucial to the maintenance of that balance. They eat a lot so keep trees and bushes in check. They recycle vegetation into fertilizer and distribute seeds via dung, so everything keeps growing. Their movements keep pathways open for other animals to use and finally, they must drink. They can dig deep into water holes, a process that benefits all creatures. I got especially fond of a small elephant family that stayed on my concession during the rainy season. I confess that remembering them is partially what motivated me to respond to your notice."

Looking again at the resume, Stuart noted, "you've been away from Africa for about five years. Why did you leave?"

Philippe thought a minute. "The short answer is that I unintendedly got caught up in the civil unrest five years ago that led to the ousting of the dictator Jean Marc Bassia. One of the perpetrators of the rebellion took refuge in the diamond production areas near my concession. His activities put the whole region into danger. In the course of an attack, I was taken hostage by some arms smugglers and was aboard their airplane when it crashed into the jungle. I was the only survivor. I recuperated by moving to the Caribbean and becoming a sailor."

"So now, you want to go back to Africa?"

"Yes, I do. I think I owe a debt to myself to make a positive contribution and I owe the creatures of Africa further recompense for having taken them so lightly in the past."

Stuart smiled, getting a nod from Susan, he extended his hand. "Sounds great Philippe. You've got the assignment."

Philippe filled out the papers for employment. Got some visa photos and took his passport along with a cover letter from ECP over to the Congolese Embassy. "Three days," they said.

T he next morning, pleased with his measure of Philippe, Stuart decided to brief him on the clandestine anti-smuggling operation underway in Kinshasa.

He began, "a local guy named Marcel Ntumbwa approached a World Wildlife Fund representative in Kinshasa about six months ago with the story that he was involved in ivory smuggling. Marcel was carefully vetted, and it did appear that he was truthful. He said upon seeing all the tusks, he realized that hundreds of elephants had died. Furthermore, they had not died for Africa, but for Chinese traders. Rather than just quit, Marcel decided to bring the problem to an organization that could stop it.

"Since we partner closely with likeminded organizations including WWF, ECP too has become involved. The master mind and financier behind the smuggling is a Chinese woman named Madame Ching. Tusks are hidden in shipping containers under false bottoms and shipped onward to various Asian destinations. The problem is that Madame pays protection to higher ups in the government and in customs, so bringing the operation down is much more than just fingering a bad Chinese lady. Marcel is now obtaining precise information on who is being paid off. Once those details are known, we'll have to decide the next step."

"Wow," Philippe exclaimed. "Africa hasn't changed. Corruption remains rife. How do I figure into this scheme?"

"You don't. The Garamba project is separate and very far away. Most of the ivory poached there leaves the continent through the east –Kenya or Tanzania - but if you do find that some is being shipped downriver, please let us know. I thought, however, that you need to know that ECP has some other irons in the fire in the Congo."

ollowing a collegial lunch in a pub near Piccadilly Circus with a group of non-governmental organization wildlife experts, Jan from WWF pulled Philippe aside.

"Philippe, Garamba was the habitat of the last known group of wild northern white rhinos. For years now we have heard of no sightings or other evidence that any of that sub-species still lives. Yet, I ask that you remain open to the possibility. The park is vast, little visited and poorly patrolled. What a great find - and feather in your cap - should you discover survivors."

"Certainly," Philippe replied. "I will keep my eyes open. I have never seen a white rhino, only blacks, but I know the name has nothing to do with color, but of lips and eating habits. All of them are big."

"Correct, white rhinos are grazers who eat grass with sort of flat mouths whereas blacks are browsers with prehensile lips so they can pull branches off bushes. As for tempcrament, whites are much more docile than blacks, so in fact they are easier to approach and thus to kill. Adult rhinos have no enemies except man and that has proven disastrous for their survival."

Philippe mulled this over afterwards. He thought it highly unlikely that any rhinos remained in northeastern Congo, but he told himself, "I'll keep an open mind."

N'djili Airport was chaotic. Arriving passengers struggled to find immigration forms all the while being badgered by "facilitators," who offered to expedite the process. Immigration authorities carefully inspected passports and visas hoping to find reason to seek a consideration of some sort. Then a presumptuous health official demanded to see a vaccination card proving immunization against yellow fever. Next passengers funneled into the stifling hot baggage hall only to wait still longer for luggage to arrive. The next gauntlet was customs, where officials scrutinized arriving persons with a practiced eye sorting out those who looked susceptible to badgering and a bribe for supposed illegal items. The final hurdle was the throng of relatives, friends, taxi drivers, expediters and others who jammed the exit.

Philippe knew the drill, kept his cool and patience as he negotiated the process. Exiting the baggage hall, he spotted a man holding a sign with his name. He introduced himself to Christopher, a driver from the World Wildlife Fund's Kinshasa office. Christopher had a relatively new white Toyota Land Cruiser with the WWF logo on the doors. He paid off the two kids who served as watchmen while Philippe stowed his luggage.

Even though it was dark, it was still early, and the city's streets were alive with people. Pedestrians abounded. Street-side bars and eateries were doing great business. Music blared loudly from speakers. Traffic was thick. Dilapidated vehicles of all sorts - cars, pickups, SUVs, mini-busses - contested for space. Although drivers were aggressive in trying to squeeze their way forward, there was a certain civility to it all and no hard feelings.

"They say you're the elephant man?" Christopher queried.

"Huh?" Philippe was startled from his gaze out the window.

"Elephant man," Christopher repeated.

"Yes, I guess so," Philippe answered. "That's what I signed up to do. Go out to Garamba Park, count the elephants and see what can be done to protect them from poachers."

"How you gonna do that?"

"We will follow the elephants around in order to count them, then patrol regularly, train and equip the rangers so they can do their job."

"You need help? I could be an elephant man too. I'm tired of these streets, not much opportunity here. I've worked for Wildlife Fund for nearly two years now. I know something about conservation programs and how they're done."

"Have you ever seen an elephant?"

"Honestly no, but we have pictures of them at the office and films. I'd like to see them for real. I have seen hippos in the river and last year I helped a lady researcher document bush meat arriving in Kin from upriver. Mostly monkeys and antelope, occasionally some bush pig or even hippo, but she freaked out when she discovered a smoked gorilla. It was pretty gruesome."

Philippe changed the topic, "So how is Kinshasa? It looks busy tonight."

"This is a happy town for many folks, but it's too many people. No good jobs. No jobs at all for most, so they mooch and thieve. Politicians and all government big men are thieves. They don't care about people, only themselves and family. Me, I got no important family. I almost got a bac at Paul VI but had to leave early. I speak and write French, but only job I find is driver/expediter for WWF. It's okay, but few opportunities for advancement. So maybe a go at being an elephant man would help."

'He is persistent,' Philippe thought. "I'll keep you in mind."

The street life thinned down as they moved into the central city where high rises and government ministries dominated. Christopher deposited him at Hotel Memling, an establishment Phillipe vaguely remembered from a visit to Kinshasa some twenty years earlier.

It was too early for bed, so after checking in Philippe headed for the bar and settled down with a cold Primus. Probably the last cold beer for a while he thought. He deflected the attentions of a very pretty girl dressed in a tight short skirt and red tube top who asked persistently if he would buy her a drink. Instead he wanted once again to mentally review his motivations for accepting this assignment and to plan the next few days. Certainly, he would check in with all the conservationist groups with offices in Kinshasa. He would also call on Ministry of Wildlife and Tourism officials as well as National Park authorities. He planned to check in with the French embassy to advise of his presence in the Congo and hopefully would chat with some of the United Nations peace keeping experts who kept tabs on the east.

hristopher picked him up at nine. Philippe spent the day consulting; first with Jan Owens, the sole representative of the Elephant Conservation Project in Kinshasa. Owens had an office co-located with the World Wildlife Fund. They went over the details of the Garamba project. ECP had agreed with the Ministry of Wildlife and Tourism to undertake a census of big game, focusing especially on elephants. How many were they? What was their range? What sort of pressure were they under from poachers and/or human neighbors? Owens explained that Garamba was truly unknown. Although designated as a national park during the colonial epoch eighty years earlier, it was never developed. Currently, it has virtually no infrastructure, just a dilapidated small headquarters village and some crude roads. When the Congo's independence came in 1960 and political chaos ensued, parks were forgotten and neglected. Even after matters settled down a bit in the seventies and eighties when Virunga Park received some support, Garamba was ignored. It was just too far off the beaten track. Matters became even worse in the nineties with the spill-over of the Rwandan genocide into eastern Zaire (now Congo again). Subsequent invaders and proxy wars pitting warlord factions against each other further troubled the east and kept Garamba isolated and unreachable.

As if internal Congolese problems weren't enough, Owens noted, Uganda's Lord's Resistance Army (LRA) was chased westward out of Uganda. Those crazies established themselves along the Sudan-Congo border and regularly ventured into Garamba. Under pressure from a combined Ugandan, American, Congolese and Central African military force, over the years LRA elements moved further into the bush, apparently mostly northward into the ungoverned border lands of South Sudan and the Central African Republic. It remained unclear as to where leader Joseph Kony and his remaining cadres were hiding. Their legacy in Garamba was poaching for meat for their own consumption, but then they discovered buyers for elephant tusks. Presently Sudanese poachers, often operating with local tribesmen, continue to pose the greatest threat to Garamba. Part of Philippe's task would be to hone in on the poaching and to devise mechanisms to halt it.

Owens confided that a key task Philippe needed to accomplish in tomorrow's meeting with the minister would be to obtain a letter specifically authorizing him to take charge of ranger training and operations. Without that sort of clout, options would be limited. Owens further advised that a suggested text for such a letter had been sent to the minister, so hopefully obtaining it would be a formality.

Philippe in turn asked about staffing, equipment, weapons and budget. Owens said ECP was flexible. What did Philippe need?

"Simplest is best, I think. Let's start small and grow as needed. I am going to want a jack of all trades for administrative duties. I doubt if suitable candidates will be in Faradja or Dungu, the towns nearest the park. WWF driver Christopher approached me. What do you think of him?"

"I like Christopher," Owens stated. "I think he has potential. He is honest, fairly smart and wants to advance. Why not sound him out to see if he fits your criteria?"

"I am also planning to ask a former colleague of mine, a Central African, who is an expert tracker to join me. This man knows more about animals and the bush than hundreds of university authorities. I don't know if he will be interested, but I want to make the offer."

"Not Congolese?" Owens mulled it over. "I suppose that far out in the bush neighboring nationality is not an impediment. However, we probably would not be able to get him a work visa through regular channels."

"I can live with that and he would too. We will have to pay him, of course, but it won't be a huge sum."

Philippe continued, "We are going to need some guns. What do the rangers carry?"

"I don't really know. Probably rusty AK-47s with little ammo, I would guess."

"Well, we'll need ammo," he paused, "at minimum for training. We'll need authorization from the ministry, but otherwise leave that to me, I see what I can scrounge up in Goma."

"Some good news from Goma," Owens added. "The Toyota Land Cruiser we've transferred from Kenya is already there and reportedly in good shape. It is right-hand drive, but that does not make much difference in the east. I should get the Congo NGO plates for it later today."

The two then spent an hour working out additional budgetary and communication details. Getting cash into outlying areas was always troublesome. There were no banks so an informal system of using a reliable shopkeeper with family links back to the capital would have to be established. Philippe had done this before so was confident he could establish a workable system.

Finally, Philippe called Christopher in for a chat. He told

him, "I am going to need an assistant in Garamba. Do you really want the position? It is a long, long way from Kinshasa."

"Yes," Christopher answered without hesitation. "I am interested."

"Well, then," Philippe stated, "tell me more about yourself? Where do you come from? What have you been doing in Kinshasa? How much education do you have?"

"Okay," Christopher replied. "I was born in Kivuka, a small village in Kongo Province, about eighty kilometers from Kinshasa. I am Kongo by tribe, second son in a family of seven - two brothers and four sisters. My grandfather, my father's father, was village chief. He was a powerful and respected man even during the time of Belgian rule. But I don't remember that, I was born much later. My father was a farmer, mostly food crops, but he achieved some success with fish. An American guy, a peace corps, helped him dig and stock a pond. Those fish produced enough money so we sons could go to school. I was a better student than my elder brother Joshua, so I advanced. I finished the local school and was sent to stay with my uncle here in Kinshasa to attend secondary. Luckily, I got into Paul VI. I was doing well there on track to a baccalaureate, when money ran out. Even before that though, I was helping with uncle's business. He runs a driving school. I started out washing cars and learned basic mechanics from his *fundi*. Uncle taught me to drive when he did not have other clients. In turn I became qualified to teach others to drive. I did that for a year all the while looking for better prospects. Finally, I landed this job driving and working with World Wildlife Fund. Uncle was sad to lose me as a teacher, but also pleased with my progress."

Philippe asked, "Are you married?"

"No, I am a single guy. There is a girl back in the village

that I was supposed to marry, but neither she nor me is interested. Girls in Kinshasa are all looking for rich men. I don't qualify. I am still young, so have time either to get rich," Christopher said with a smile, "or find the right girl."

"Tell me about school," Phillipe said, "for example, how is your math?"

"I liked all subjects, including math and science, but I liked literature best."

Philippe pulled a newspaper from his briefcase. "Let me give you a little test. Read this opinion piece from **La Monde** newspaper and then tell me in your own words what it is about."

Christopher took the proffered paper, furrowed his brow and read. Five minutes later he said, "OK." Philippe nodded. Christopher began, "It deals with the question of division of powers and responsibilities between levels of government in France. Mayors of cities reject the imposition of rules and regulations by the central government in Paris as ordered by prefects. The case in point was local decision in Marseilles not to accept a national ban on religious head scarves for Muslim girls and women in schools. Both sides to the dispute claim constitutional justification for their stance. La Monde supports the mayor's position."

"Very good," Philippe complimented. "Does Congo face any similar problems?"

"Well, not over head scarves. I think in the modern political and legal arena in Congo the President and his government are supreme. Mayors do have authorities over markets, local taxes and fees and such, but even there can be overturned by the government. But still today in villages and rural zones, local law and custom often prevail; mostly I suppose on account of the absence of national authorities. For example, my grandfather ran the village as it had been done for generations, His successor does it the same."

"Good point," Philippe acknowledged. He continued, "okay, Christopher, thanks for talking to me, I am ready to give you a trial as my assistant. You must be ready to spend months at a time in an isolated national park. Can you do that?"

Christopher kept his poise. "Yes, I can do the job. I can be an elephant man."

Philippe's grin was as big as Christopher's. They shook hands on the deal.

Ndomazi settled back into his low-slung chair carefully situated under the burgeoning shade of a huge mango tree. Hard packed bare earth stretched out for dozens of meters around him in the time-honored fashion of an African village. Bare ground was sanitary and kept bugs at bay. It was mid-morning, but already hot. It surely would get hotter as the sun climbed higher into the azure sky. Village sounds wafted softly from surrounding huts. Chickens squawked, dogs barked, flies buzzed, a baby wailed. Ndomazi could hear the well pump creaking in the distance as womenfolk pumped water and chattered as they did. No rain today, he thought. Physically small, even wizened, Ndomazi was an elder of indeterminate age, maybe in his fifties or sixties. He looked over this shoulder at his concrete block house. It was by far the biggest and the only concrete dwelling in the village, both aspects symbolized his stature as patriarch. A red blooming bougainvillea vine was creeping up one corner. It's much better here than in the capital, Ndomazi told himself. I did my time there, but at heart I am a bush man. I need to be here in the village or better yet scouting the hunting grounds.

As he sat reminiscing about earlier times, Grace, a grandniece, appeared at his side offering a cup of tea. It was hot, milky, sugary and smoky - just as he liked it. He thanked her politely and was grateful that some of his extended family shared simple village life. His two children, who had accompanied him on the move to the capital, became educated and enamored of city life. His oldest Philippe, whom he named for his old patron, had a good job with a timber exporting firm. His daughter Marie married last year and was soon expecting her first child. Nonetheless, Ndomazi decided that his time in the city was done. He resigned his special army commission and went home. He had no regrets. It was the right thing to do. He had done his best to train soldiers in bush craft and almost all had learned something, but really to be a tracker, he concluded one had to be immersed in the wilds. After a few years in the army, it was time to resign honorably. So, he did. His senior wife Angela readily agreed. She too wanted to return to her home village.

As he sat, he remembered that his village was not always so peaceful. According to the stories, long before his time white men marched into the village. They carried rifles and had many African soldiers under their command. In the Sango language of the region the whites came to be called *mjou*. Ndomazi later learned that was the human prefix of '*m*' being placed before a contraction of *bonjour*, so whites were humans who said bonjour. The name may have been logical, but whites were not. They demanded food, shelter, women, labor and ivory. The region did not harbor many elephants and villagers rarely hunted such large beasts, so there was no ivory to be had. But labor was demanded. The whites said their *societe* had been granted rights to the whole area. The company would plant cotton and men must come to work the fields. A levy of the number of men was placed on each village and was enforced brutally against the village if the requisite number of men did not report. In one nearby instance to ensure flagging cooperation the soldiers took all the women and children of a village hostage and locked them in a warehouse for days without food or water. Dozens died. Surrounding villages took note and met their labor quotas.

Even as this was going on, the whites said the government required more men to build an iron trail to the ocean. Again, men were rounded up, this time including Ndomazi's father's father Mutomba and his brother Nkuti. Two hundred conscripts from the *societe's* concession were chained together and marched to the big river where they were loaded onto a huge flat canoe pushed by a noisy smoky boat. Mutomba and his brother were terrified but as young men also curious about this new world. The overcrowded barge pushed slowly down stream. Water was plentiful but there was almost no food. Within days it came to a city, Mutomba remembered it was called Bangui, where the captives were put into a compound and fed. The Africans who guarded them laughed at the country bumpkins and told them tales of the horrors of work on the iron trail, primitive camps, little food, forced labor, lifting, digging, carting rocks in the unremitting heat, disease and the lash took their toll. The guards said few would survive. Guards reported that the captives would be loaded onto a bigger barge for the two-week trip to Brazzaville. That mystical place was the beginning of the iron trail, the Congo-Ocean railway.

The brothers conferred. They had seen enough and heard too much. They plotted escape. Mutomba believed that jumping into the river would be best. It would be a desperate act. They were poor swimmers, but perhaps could catch a floating limb or tree. Nkuti reluctantly agreed with his brother's plan. So, the plot was set. The next day the men were herded like cattle onto a barge with high fences around the outside. The guards from the compound armed with rifles took positions on towers surrounding the men. Mutomba would relate how he carefully watched which of the guards were attentive and which were not. He selected a spot. He also confided to a fellow villager the need for a diversion. His friend agreed. In the stupor of the late afternoon, he whispered to Nkuti that it was time. He nodded to his accomplice who loudly began a raucous brawl at the far end of the barge. All the guards turned their attention to the fight. The two brothers scurried up the fencing and slipped under the looped barbed wire at the top. At that moment they were spotted but they dropped over the edge into the muddy river water. Mutomba recalled plunging into the depths, being sucked and swirled as the push boat moved over him. The thrum of the engine filled his ears, he half glanced at a large turning propeller. Suddenly he was thrust upwards. He gasped for air once before being sucked under again in the boat's eddy. Stunned and buffeted, Mutomba again rose to the surface. The boat was now downstream moving steadily away. Several guards stood on the back of the boat aiming their rifles at him. Mutomba saw puffs of smoke as they fired, but he was already out of range. Somehow Mutomba made it towards shore. He grabbed an overhanging branch and held on until he could gather his strength and move to the bank. He looked anxiously for Nkuti but saw no sign of him.

Mutomba pulled himself through the mud and struggled to stand. Gathering his strength, he hollered "Nkuti" again and again. There was no answer. Mutomba searched the river waters but saw no sign. He sloshed through the mud at the water's edge, but still nothing. Sobbing, he fell, bereft of his brother - his younger sibling whom he was sworn to protect. He failed. How could he answer to their father? Nkuti was no more, swept - Mutomba was convinced - to his death in the churning brown waters of the great river. As he sat, Mutomba blamed himself for the foolish idea of jumping from the boat. After another hour of sloshing his way along the muddy bank, Mutomba gave up. He sat again to decide what to do next. He had no idea where he was, remembering only that Bangui was upstream. He did not recall seeing any habitation from the barge. There was a muddy, occasionally stony shelf just at the river's edge. Behind that a ten-foot bank rose abruptly to a dense jungle of greenery. Trees taller than he could imagine stretched to the sky. The understory was so dense with bushes and vines that a man could hardly push through. Birds cried from the treetops. A troop of monkeys joined in as they hooted at Mutomba from their leafy perches. 'If I go in there,' Mutomba mused to himself, 'I'll just disappear.' He concluded that he must move upstream as best he could along the verge of the water. Bidding Nkuti a final farewell, Mutomba asked for his forgiveness, then retraced his steps along the riverbank and beyond.

It was a slog moving through the mud, climbing over drifted trees, fighting through vines but finding odd patches of sand or rocks that eased movement. Mutomba walked until dark, then huddled in the roots of a downed tree for the night. It was not cold, but was humid and damp, a far cry from the drier climate of home. He heard snorting and honking from a pod of hippos nearby but felt protected by the wood around him. A drenching rain fell during the night, but the day dawned bright and clear. His spirits buoyed, Mutomba set out again.

After hours of movement, about mid-morning, Mutomba spotted an obviously human made clearing on the far bank. A tendril of smoke curled up into the sky from a little hut. However, the river was several hundred meters wide and he had no intention of trying to swim across. Mutomba reached a point directly across from the dwelling and yelled. He saw no movement. He yelled again. Still nothing. Resigned to being ignored, Mutomba sat on a log and reviewed his options. He knew there was no guarantee that if anyone was present that they would help. Finally, he concluded it was best just to move on. He trudged onward. Just then, he saw a small pirogue - a dugout canoe - floating slowly downstream towards him. A single man paddled. Mutomba waved frantically and the stranger approached. Without beaching the pirogue, the paddler returned Mutomba's greeting. The two did not have much language in common, but Mutomba pantomimed that he had fallen off the big boat and needed to go upstream. The young fisherman took pity, took Mutomba on board and across to his camp.

There they shared a pot of fish stew - Mutomba was ravenous - as they sought to communicate. Mutomba understood that the fisherman would paddle him upriver until they reached a village, from there trails led to the city. They set out by early afternoon. Mutomba was careful to steady himself in the small boat whose sides were scarcely inches above the water, but his guide was skillful and stayed in the calmer shallows near the bank. Just before dark, they arrived at a beach where several bigger pirogues were pulled far up onto the sand. "My village," the fisherman confirmed. He led Mutomba to a house where he introduced Mutomba to the elders. They indicated he could stay the night.

The next morning a boy showed Mutomba the trail that led through gardens and forests to the city. Ndomazi remembered his grandfather saying the city was bigger than any place he had ever seen or even thought of. He avoided going near the prison compound down near the docks but reveled in the wide streets and solidly built houses and buildings.

The African neighborhoods were row after confused row of traditional mud houses with grass roofs, but already there was a plethora of various tribesmen present from all corners of the territory. Mutomba was careful not to draw attention. He was just another wandering tribesman. He kept an ear cocked for the words around him. He fixed on two men standing before a vegetable stand speaking his native tongue. He greeted them in kind and was greatly relieved with an enthusiastic welcome of kindred tribesmen from the east. Mutomba admitted he was newly arrived in the city, destitute and at a complete loss of what to do next. The three traded information about families, clans, personages, villages and places in the east. Once they established a common data base the two led Mutomba to their abode - a ramshackle shack in a densely packed neighborhood. They assured him, their cousin from home, he could stay while he got on his feet. One other fellow easterner shared the dwelling.

Ndomazi recalled his grandfather telling of his time in Bangui. With guidance from his hosts, Mutomba found work as a menial laborer building city streets. It was hard work, but better grandfather said than slaving away on the iron trail. All the city folk kept alert to the possibility of being dragooned and sent south, but apparently their labor was needed in the new capital. Paid a pittance, yet it was enough to contribute to the common pot and to put away a few coins for a hoped trip home. Mutomba chatted with and listened to fellow workers and soon gained a suitable capacity in Sangho, the emerging lingua franca of the territory. With increased fluency Mutomba learned about city ways. First was to steer clear of all *mjous*. Their power over blacks was total and their capriciousness unpredictable. He had no doubts about either aspect because not only did he witness beatings and arrests for the slightest of offences in the city, he remembered the atrocities committed against villagers back home. Although he found the city - the markets and the burgeoning neighborhoods - fascinating, Mutomba yearned to go home. After almost a year in Bangui, he was able finally to book passage on a barge going upriver. The boat delivered him back to the port where his ill-fated journey had begun. From there Mutomba walked for five days retracing his steps to home.

Welcomed as the prodigal son he was, Mutomba had the sad duty of reporting his brother's death. His kin mourned the loss but accepted it as unchangeable fate. Life went on. By then quite wary of anything having to do with *mjous*, Mutomba abandoned his village and established an isolated homestead deep in the bush. Eventually he would marry and raise a family. Over the years his homestead would grow into a village.

Growing up Ndomazi heard his grandfather's tale of the trip, the river and the city, many times. But the old man was more than a storyteller; he was an accomplished hunter and tracker. He took young Ndomazi under his wing and taught him bush craft. How to read the signs, find the tracks, listen to the wind, sniff the smells, hear the birds - everything, Grandfather instructed him, told a tale. He had to piece it together, so it made sense.

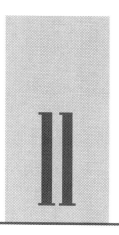

fter a long day in the office - talking to Owens, briefing Christopher on his duties and making lists of equipment needed, Philippe needed respite. As the day was beginning to fade, he strode out of the hotel and turned down towards the river. He passed through a pleasant tree filled neighborhood of big houses encircled by high walls. Razor wire curled along the top of most. A row of houses blocked access to the river. Damp and moldy smells wafted in the light breeze. Philippe could see water hyacinths floating by on the current. He noticed the lights and a few skyscrapers of Brazzaville on the far bank. Philippe calculated that the river must be about five miles wide at this point, just before it narrowed and tumbled violently down a series of steep inclines creating treacherous impassable rapids in the hundred miles from Stanley Pool to the sea. A bit irritated that he could not actually stand on the bank, Philippe slowly turned and headed back. He had not gone far when a black Toyota sedan abruptly pulled in front of him. Two men jumped out, grabbed him quickly. Philippe thought briefly about fighting, but decided he was outnumbered. He surmised it was a robbery, but he did not have much on him. He did not struggle as they forced him into the car. The door shut with a thud. Once there, the man in front turned to him flashed a badge and said, "we are police officers. You were walking in a prohibited zone. You are now in our custody. What are you doing here?"

Philippe replied, "I was taking an evening stroll down to see your famous river. I did not know this was forbidden. I saw no signs to that effect. I am a visitor to Congo. I just arrived two days ago."

Philippe's response was hardly listened to. The lead officer stayed with his ploy. "Nonsense, everyone knows that movement near the presidential compound is forbidden." He pointed vaguely down the road. "You are guilty, so we must arrest you, book you and throw you in jail, until your embassy can sort you out." He smiled, "that may take several days at best."

He waited. Philippe remained calm recognizing that this was only a shake-down - the price and bargaining would come next.

The policeman added, "perhaps in order to avoid that, we can come to an arrangement. About 300 euros should do it."

Philippe decided to play. "Sorry but I don't have that kind of money. I am a simple conservationist here on a shoestring budget. I am supposed to go east in a day or two to Garamba Park to count elephants. I am scheduled to meet with the minister of tourism and wildlife tomorrow. I'm sure he would be disappointed to learn that I did not experience Kinshasa's warmest hospitality." Let them stew on that Philippe thought.

"Ha," the cop retorted, "tomorrow you will be in jail, so don't make useless threats about the minister."

"Well, perhaps we can come to an arrangement. As I said I am an elephant expert, particularly an expert in elephant sexual activity. You know that elephants are big. The bull male has the largest penis in the world. It is over a meter long. When aroused it sometimes even drags on the ground. The bull becomes so obsessed with sex that fluid drips out of holes near his eyes and semen drips from his dong. He will fight any other bull that challenges his access to females. He will use his trunk to sort out the girls, then mount the ready ones, time and again. None can resist him. He is too powerful and too crazed.

"My research has focused on this. What makes the bull so potent? Over time, and I must say often in very dangerous situations, I isolated the essence of what empowers him. If a man were to swallow this essence, he too would become an unrelenting sex machine capable of servicing many women. Such a man's reputation as a lover would become legend."

Philippe paused. He noticed that the three policemen were captivated by their imaginations. He continued, "I have a small sample of that essence with me, perhaps instead of euros I could give you each a dose?"

"Yes, yes," the three agreed in unison. "We'll take it."

They drove the elephant expert to his hotel. The senior man went with him to his room but acceded to Philippe's request to wait in the hall. Philippe quickly crushed three vitamin pills and dumped the residue into hotel envelopes. He slipped these furtively to the cop. "Don't take this until you are completely ready to wreak sexual havoc." The policeman nodded affirmatively and rushed off to share the loot with his co-conspirators.

Philippe sat and had a good laugh. He guessed that the placebo effect would pay dividends and he would never see the three again. However, caution prevailed, and he went to the desk and changed his room.

The day was heavy on account of rain just before dawn. Nonetheless, Philippe ate breakfast on the terrace as the sun struggled to break through the low clouds. His meeting with the minister was scheduled for late morning, meanwhile Philippe scratched out a letter to Ndomazi, tracker, guide and friend who had worked with him for years in the Central African Republic. Philippe did not have an address for Ndomazi but having looked up an address on the internet for Jean Mbaito, currently CAR's Minister of Defense, he planned to post the letter to him for forwarding to Ndomazi. Mbaito would certainly know how to contact the tracker. Satisfied with his plan, Philippe bought stamps from the desk and was promised that the letter would be mailed that morning at the central post office. Philippe recognized that this was at best a fragile communications link, but no other means of contact came to mind. I will have to be patient, he told himself.

Owens joined him for the call on the minister. The ministry was housed in a rundown three-story building along with ministries of information and youth and sports. The courtyard and the hallways were full of people - those with appointments, those wanting appointments, those wanting jobs, wandering ministry staff and other hangers-on. There was even a football team of teenagers in matching blue jerseys, apparently waiting for an award of some sort. Owens led the way through the crowds, up the stairs to the end of a long corridor. The two conservationists knocked politely and entered the outer office of the minister. A secretary greeted them warmly, advised that the minister was expecting them and asked them to sit. Two sofas and several straight back chairs filled the office. Only one place was free. The secretary motioned for a petitioner to vacate his spot to give the two foreigners space.

The secretary spoke on her phone. Told the visitors, "It will be just a minute."

Owens cynically whispered, "minutes or hours." They waited patiently while conversations among the other supplicants resumed quietly.

Before long the minister's door opened and a tall well-dressed man stepped out. "Mr. Owens," he greeted Jan, "and this must be Mr. Darman. I am Abdel Gumba, the minister's chief of staff. Please come in." He gestured towards the door.

The minister, the Honorable Moise Tumba, rose from behind his desk, walked around to greet them. He too was a tall individual, well turned out in a dark suit and pink tie and sporting a thin goatee. He had a firm handshake.

"Welcome, welcome," he began. "I am so pleased that the Garamba project is falling into place. Mr. Darman, I have read your resume and am impressed with your expertise. You seem to be just right for the assignment."

The minister continued, "I have asked the director of parks to join us. He should be here soon." He cast a glance at Gumba, who immediately advised, "Sir, he is on his way."

"Up until now," the minister stated, "we have concentrated resources and attention on the rehabilitation of Virunga National Park, on the gorilla sanctuary of Kahuzi-Biega and increasingly on the bonobo sanctuary in the Ituri Forrest.

All of those areas have great potential for tourism and so can ultimately be expected to pay their own way. Outlying regions, however, like Garamba have traditionally supported quantities of game, especially elephants and rhinos, and so must be preserved until their tourist potential can be realized. I am told that the rhinos are probably gone from Garamba, but thousands of elephants remain. This project, a joint undertaking between my government and the Elephant Conservation Project is designed to protect them and to preserve the park."

Philippe nodded in support. He has his spiel down pat, he thought. Just then another Congolese official walked in. "Sorry, I'm late, Minister," he apologized. Ignoring the apology, honorable Tumba ordered, "So Jacques, tell them what we have at Garamba."

"Not much," the Parks director replied, "as Mr. Owens knows, there is a park headquarters with a few buildings. Several vehicles are in the inventory, but I don't know if any work. Twelve rangers are assigned to the park and most, I am told, are there. However, there is not presently a director, nor has there been for some years. The last one was shot and wounded by the Lords' Resistance Army. He quit and we have not yet named a replacement. I was hoping that Mr. Darman would act in that capacity for the next few months."

The Congolese team looked expectantly at the visitors. Philippe scrunched his brow. "I would be pleased to take charge of the park's security and anti-poaching efforts. That's what I have signed on to do, but I am not competent to get into the tourism business. However, I understand that aspect of what's possible in the park has not yet arrived. Can we proceed with that clarification?"

"Indeed," the minister agreed, "we can. Jacques, draw up

the appropriate appointment papers for my signature. And thanks Mr. Darman and Mr. Owens, for your support."

Back in the corridor winding their way out of the building, Owens said, "well Philippe, we got a green light. I hope it is not more than you can do."

"I am satisfied. At best they won't be meddling, at least for a while. I only trust that the minimal resources the ministry provides for the park, especially pay for the rangers, won't be disrupted."

Back in his office Minister Tumba told Abdel and Jacques, "okay, we have turned Garamba over to foreigners. If knowledge of this becomes widespread it will be politically unpopular, but we don't have the resources that conservation NGOs do. Let's see what they can accomplish."

In the afternoon Philippe called on the UN Peacekeeping Mission in Congo (UNPKC). He spoke with two officials - a Norwegian army captain and a young Belgian woman who monitored humanitarian operations in Ituri Province. The captain provided a concise briefing of the military situation in the east, especially the northeast. It had been a turbulent twenty years as regional politics from Uganda and Rwanda mixed with local tribal antagonisms creating an unhealthy stew of competition, corruption and unchecked violence. Most of the violence generated in the various flare-ups had been confined to areas south of Garamba Park where politically motivated attacks and reprisals combined to kill thousands and strangle the economy. Except for exploitation of coltan and gold, which added incentive to the various struggles, the modern economy had collapsed. Local transportation diminished, educational and health services evaporated as the troubled region regressed across the board to a more primitive state.

Garamba, however, had endured its own plague - that of the Lord's Resistance Army. For about five years their predations, specific attacks aimed at isolated homesteads, rural villages and even the region's two largest towns, Dungu and Faradje, caused thousands of people to move to government supervised displaced persons camps. UNPKC arrived to calm the situation and protect the camps. However, once the US/Ugandan military chased the LRA away into South Sudan and CAR, the camps closed, and the displaced people returned home. Subsequently, UNPKC downsized its operation in Dungu and had now mostly left the region. The captain stated that UNPKC did, however, still send a patrol on a northern circuit about once a month.

UNPKC east was headquartered in Goma with a subordinate field operation based in Bunia. Philippe asked for introductions to the commands. The captain readily agreed to advise his colleagues of Elephant Conservation Project's undertaking, Philippe's presence and mission in Garamba.

The young lady, a no-nonsense brunette, elaborated on the economic, social, health and educational situation. "It's dire," she said. "Most services have simply ceased to function. Where there are operating schools and clinics, it is because the local communities, often aided by missionaries, do it themselves. Several international NGOs set up operations at the camps near Dungu during the LRA emergency, but as that wound down, most have departed. I believe that *Medecins Sans Frontieres* still has staff there. Believe me, if it wasn't for MSF there would be almost no higher end medical services anywhere in eastern Congo!"

What am I getting myself into? Philippe wondered as he listened carefully to the briefers.

Since the French Embassy was not far from the UN

compound, Philippe stopped there, filled out a form registering as a French citizen in the Congo and giving his address as Garamba Park headquarters, Uele Province. The French consular official who reviewed the form clucked softly in dismay mentioning that France advised citizens to stay out of eastern Congo. France could provide no help when troubles ensued. Philippe rejoined that he understood the official advice and the policy. He said he did not intend to get into any trouble, only to count some elephants.

The street, it was really more of a path, was dark. It was after nine. Shadows danced as clouds passed under a half moon. Marcel knew the way. He twisted and turned to avoid the potholes and trash piles. There was no electricity in Ngaliema, one of the city's biggest and poorest slums. But here and there feeble kerosene lantern light filtered through the cracks or half-closed windows of the shacks and shanties that lined the route. Passing the empty roughhewn stands of a daily fruit and vegetable market, Marcel heard the snoring of a night guard or a homeless man, probably the same person. Radio music from behind closed doors bounced softly through the cooling, but still very humid, night air. Marcel carefully skirted the perpetual mud around the communal standpipe. The ever-present stench of the nearby public latrines indicated he was close to home.

Marcel slipped his key into the padlock and snapped it open. He pushed the door back and placed the lock on the shelf just inside. Moving by memory, he found the candle stub and matches in their place on the table. The flickering candle showed a small room about four meters square. It held two single beds separated by a cloth hanging. Each bed had a thin foam mat on top. Marcel was not surprised to note that his cousin Wendo, with whom he shared the abode, was not there. Otherwise the lock would not have been locked. There were two chairs, one a straight back and the other a low-slung lounger typical of a Congolese village. A small table and a cupboard completed the furniture.

Marcel closed the door. With a sigh he settled into the lounger. After work he had walked the five miles or so home, stopping only for a bite at a street front cafe along the way. He was getting scared, fearful that his resolve to oust the ivory smugglers was waning. Maybe I'd best just stop, he thought. He reviewed what he knew. Ivory was transported downriver from Mbandaka under false floors of containers filled with sawn hardwoods, mostly *sapelli* and mahogany. Those special containers were mixed with others in the company transit yard, then forwarded without customs scrutiny on to China - Taipei or Macau. The papers for apparently all of the company's exports were complete and properly signed and sealed by relevant authorities. Marcel had told his contact at the Wildlife Fund about how the ivory moved and to what consignees, but so far, he was not able to determine who authorized the export documents that facilitated the smuggling. They urged him to keep digging.

A knock on the door aroused Marcel from a half slumber. "Marcel, it's me Moussa, from work." Before he could stand, the door burst open and three men rushed in. Two grabbed him, pinned his arms to his side. The larger man clamped a stinking cloth over his face and his struggle slowed. The smaller man, his features hidden under a black hoodie, slipped a wire garrote around Marcel's neck and pulled tight. It was over in seconds, Marcel was dead.

Telling his conspirators to wait outside, the smaller man then drew a knife. Prying the dead man's mouth open, he reached in and severed his tongue. He pocketed the grisly bloody relic in a plastic bag. The man pulled Marcel's phone from his pocket, blew out the candle, then hustled away. The killers paused briefly to see if their crime caused any reaction. All was quiet.

Wendo came home about an hour later. He had just spent several delightful hours with his girlfriend, but she always ordered him out by midnight. Wendo noted that the door was unlocked, so knew Marcel was home. He came in, closed and barred the door, intending just to sneak quietly to bed. In the dark he stumbled upon something. Reaching down he felt a body. He flashed his phone which revealed the gruesome scene. His cousin lying dead on the floor with blood pooled under his head having dripped from his mouth.

An anguished cry of grief escaped from his throat. Wendo immediately linked the killing in his mind to Marcel's efforts to uncover a smuggling ring. He had told Marcel that effort was unwise, but Marcel was determined. Although fearing that he might be next, Wendo knew he must report the murder. He dashed out, down to the sector chief's house several hundred meters away. Banging on the door he roused the chief who in turn called the police on his cell phone. The chief required that Wendo stay with him until the police arrived. It being night in the slum, that could take a while.

Ji knocked softly on the door. "Enter," came the command. He slid through the portal. In the dim light she was sitting in a cloud of opium smoke. Her eyes, however, were sharp and piercing. Ji approached and bowed. "It is done, Madame. Just as you ordered. Here is his phone." Ji proffered the device.

"And his tongue?" she demanded. "I must have the traitor's tongue."

"Yes, it is here too. In this sack." He gave that to her as well.

She coughed and rasped, "well done. Now leave me."

Ji nodded and slowly backed out of the room.

Madame Ching eyed the bloody sack. Slowly opening it she slid the severed tongue out onto a cutting board she had positioned next to her chair. Picking up a sharp knife she cut a sliver off. She transferred the bloody morsel to her mouth and swallowed quickly. She steeled herself not to gag and didn't. A shot of whiskey, she preferred Johnnie Walker Black, washed it down. The remainder of the tongue would go down the privy.

Madame congratulated herself on having neutralized the traitor. I have taken his power. Even so, she recognized that evidence against Marcel was slim. He had just been nosing around too much, looking at documents he didn't normally see and asking questions. Perhaps he did not realize that she was always watching. Madame trusted that his phone would produce contacts. Meanwhile, once the current shipment was away, she would hold back the next one.

N galiema Police Sub-Station report of death of Marcel Ntumbwa

1. At 1235 hours June 15, 2018, the station received a call from Solomon Nguta, chief of sector 17, reporting a death in his sector, presumably a murder.
2. Constables Dinda and Bomkobo went to the scene within the hour, a room located about fifty meters from communal standpipe 17. They verified that a victim lay dead on the floor. The constables secured the scene until day light.
3. Inspector Bahuti arrived at the crime site at 0900. He verified the death of Marcel Ntumbwa apparently by strangulation, probably by a wire around the neck. This was later verified by the medical examiner.
4. Ntumbwa's wallet containing several hundred francs and his identity card was found in his pocket. His phone was missing. Otherwise, the house had not been ransacked. One obvious item of value, a radio, remained in place on a shelf.
5. Marcel Ntumbwa, 24 was not married. He lived in the room with his cousin Wendo Yambuya. They had been renting the room for the past two years. Ntumbwa was employed by Best African Hardwoods, Ltd. Yambuya is a part time taxi driver.

6. Yambuya said he returned home about 2355 on June 13 from having spent the evening with his girlfriend, an alibi which she and others in her household confirm. The door was unlocked so he entered and stumbled upon his cousin's dead body. Yambuya ran to Sector Chief Nguta.

7. Yambuya could give no reason why Ntumbwa was targeted and killed or who might have done the deed. He said Ntumbwa was not involved sexually or romantically with anyone at this time.

8. Ntumbwa's supervisor at Best African Hardwoods, James Ouygi, was sorry to learn of the death. He said Ntumbwa was a good worker, punctual and reliable. His job was to track the whereabouts of containers in the yard, to coordinate with transport arrangers in order to ensure containers went where they were supposed to go. Ouygi said to his knowledge Ntumbwa had no problems or enemies at work. He added that in accordance with law and policy, the company would provide a compensation package to the bereaved family.

9. The medical examiner reported that the victim's tongue had been removed. It was not found on the premises. The examiner said this type of mutilation was very unusual and it tended to rule out jealousy/ revenge as a motive, because in such cases genitals were cut off and stuck in the victim's mouth.

10. The victim's body was released to the family.

11. The investigation continues.

hilippe found Owens and WWF chief Rentyns deep in conversation. "You should know this." Owens waved towards a chair, "sit down. We learned late this morning that our confidential source tracking the ivory smuggling ring, a man named Marcel, was killed...most certainly murdered last night. We presume he was killed on account of his activities, but don't know that for sure. A guy who identified himself as Marcel's cousin called Marcel's contact here at WWF to advise of the killing. The cousin, who did not give his name, was apparently quite agitated. He said we too should be afraid."

Rentyns added, "Timothy, who was the point of contact, is quite shaken. I am too. Marcel's death will surely scuttle our inquiry and perhaps rebound in negative fashion to other conservation activities."

Philippe asked, "what have the police said? Has the crime been reported? Has the motive, if it was the smuggling, come out?"

"We simply don't know. We deem it best not to ask as that would tip our hand and confirm our involvement, both to the police and to the perpetrators."

"So, we are stuck?" Philippe summarized.

"Not completely," Rentyns replied. "I will ask a friend, a discreet journalist to poke around, but a murder in a Kinshasa slum is not big news."

Afterwards Philippe mulled over the remark, "not big news." Maybe not for the bigger world, but for Marcel it certainly was. Philippe could not help but consider that Marcel was a martyr for a bigger cause. One that he decided was important, that of protection of elephants. Jill too had died for that cause. Her death in the CAR some years ago was tragic. Marcel's was too. He acknowledged that like Jill's death, Marcel's would be noted only in passing, and mostly by friends and family. Jill's murder was part of his motivation. Now he would add Marcel, whom he never even met, as an extra incentive to do right in Garamba. These are dangerous times Philippe concluded. Money and greed overrule common sense. I will have to be extra careful in Congo's lawless east.

O wens and a driver deposited Philippe and Christopher at the entrance of N'djili Airport. "Good luck guys," he said in parting. "Stay in touch."

"You bet," Philippe jested, "we'll take good care of your laptop and satellite phone." More seriously he added, "you stay safe here."

Although Christopher had been to N'djili many times, he had never been through it. Philippe guided him through check-in, security and waiting. The flight east to Goma was more or less on time. It was an old Antonov complete with Russian pilots, but it was the only transportation between the capital and the east. Although most boarding passengers appeared to be Congolese, there were a dozen Caucasians, whom Philippe guessed were UN or NGO personnel.

Takeoff was uneventful albeit very noisy. "I trust she'll hold together," Philippe muttered. Christopher was oblivious to the comment. He marveled looking out the window as the teeming city disappeared below, soon to be dwarfed by the great brown snake of the Congo River. That too faded as the aircraft passed into the clouds. When it dropped back down some two hours later, Christopher was glued to the sight of glistening blue Lake Kivu surrounded by green volcanic peaks stretching up to the sky. Almost before he could soak it all in, they landed with a thump.

Christopher quickly proved his worth in lining up a

respectable taxi that carried them to the once prestigious Lake Hotel. It was a bit dowdy, but had a wonderful view looking out over flower filled gardens to the lake beyond. Since they had an afternoon available, Philippe wanted to collect the Toyota and begin purchasing supplies.

First stop was the Golden Emporium - H.R. Patel and sons, proprietors - as the faded sign said. A middle-aged Indian gentleman greeted them as they entered, "welcome, welcome, what can I do for you this fine day. We have all types of goods, perfect for NGO operations. Certainly, we can please."

"Many thanks," Philippe responded. "Are you H.R. Patel?"

"Gracious no. He was my grandfather, but we grandsons carry on his honorable tradition."

"Fine, I am Philippe Darman, representative of the Elephant Conservation Project. I understand you have a Toyota Land Cruiser for me."

"Ah, indeed, indeed. It is just out back. I will just be getting the key." Mr. Patel led the way. There it was: white with ECP emblems on the doors. It looked to be in good shape. They kicked the tires, fired it up. Christopher was leery of the right-hand drive, but Philippe assured him he would get the hang of it quickly. Patel noted with pride, "freshly washed!" The three retreated to the office. "Papers to sign," Patel noted. He called for tea while they read and signed. Philippe advised they were off to take charge of Garamba Park. "So, what else do you need," the merchant queried greedily.

"We have a long list," Philippe noted, "but I also need some reputable guns and ammunition. Can you help there?"

"Oh, oh, guns are always trouble. AK-47s are easily obtained, but better weapons are hard to come by."

"I won't need AKs but will need quite a lot of AK ammo.

I have a government issued requisition order for the ammo, so am quite legitimate."

Patel looked relieved.

Philippe continued, "for myself, I require a good hunting rifle and perhaps a nice shotgun."

Patel frowned. "I have not been able to stock good guns for some years, but I do still have some rounds." He wrinkled his brow, "you know there is an old Belge here in Goma, who was a famous big game hunter in his day. My grandfather was his chief supplier. I offered to buy his weapons several years ago, but he refused to sell saying he did not want them to fall in the wrong hands. Maybe he will sell to you. Shall I give him a tinkle?"

"Yes, please do."

Alex Delcroix said he was free and invited Philippe to visit. Following Patel's directions, driving very cautiously, Christopher found the house. "This is not so hard," he commented.

Philippe went in alone. A houseman met him at the door and ushered him out to a terrace overlooking the lake. A grey-haired man rose stiffly from his chair but stood erect. "Alex Delcroix," he stated introducing himself. Philippe replied in kind. "So why does Patel think I need to see you, something about Garamba I take it. I used to hunt up that way years ago."

Philippe explained his mission, to census and protect elephants as well as other game in the park. He noted that he was named interim director, so had full authority of the government. Philippe thought his personal hunting background would help sway the old man. So, he spoke of his years in the Central African Republic. Delcroix interrupted when Philippe named his mentor Claude Mossier. "Mossier, huh, I knew him. Excellent shot and a good bloke besides. We went after big jumbos together once, just south of the Haut Mbomu river."

Philippe finally got to the point. "Even though my park rangers have AK-47s, I need something better. The hassle of bringing guns across borders was just too much to organize in the time available, so I am looking to purchase locally. Patel said you might be inclined to sell."

"Interesting. That scoundrel has been watching me for years. His granddad was a right proper gentleman, a standard that the current proprietors have yet to reach. So, what kind of guns do you want?"

"I need a heavy hunting weapon, one capable of stopping an elephant. I am not going to be hunting, but if we are near them, I must be prepared. Secondly, a decent shotgun, again not for hunting, but for close in work as needed."

"And for protection," Delcroix added.

"Yes, that too."

"Let's take a look." He rose slowly. "I used to keep them in a gun safe, but now I keep them much more securely locked away." He led the way into the house, down the hall into a spare bedroom. The closet had been reinforced with concrete and a steel vault door hung on it. "I got the door from a bank that went under." The old hunter spun the dial and swung the vault open. Inside was a marvelous collection of weaponry, easily two dozen classic hunting guns. Philippe gasped. Delcroix chuckled at his astonishment. "Yep, good stuff here." He paused to admire his collection. "For a heavy gun, this Mauser 98 will probably do the trick." He lifted the gun off the rack and handed it to Philippe. ".375, bolt action, superb telescopic sight. And to boot Patel still carries ammo for it." Philippe weighed the weapon. He had a Weatherley Vanguard previously but knew the Mauser and its solid reputation. This one was a beauty. "And for a shotgun, this Remington 1100 would probably serve." It too was a beautiful piece of work and the care its owner gave it was evident in its shine.

"Then, you will sell?" Philippe queried.

"Yep," the old man replied with a grin, "sounds like a good cause...and you were a friend of Mossier's."

They shook on the deal.

orking with Patel, Philippe and Christopher assembled all the gear from the list - cots, sleeping bags, mosquito nets, cooking and eating utensils, jerry cans, solar panels, batteries, etc. plus a supply of dry and canned goods. Certainly foodstuffs, including seasonal vegetables and fruit, would be available near the park, but it was good to have staples and a reserve. Patel also produced ammo for AK-47s and for Philippe's newly acquired weapons. Mr. Patel was very pleased that he fostered the deal for the guns. "Very, very, nice," he congratulated himself.

Philippe introduced himself to the UNPKC authorities. As promised the Norwegian captain in Kinshasa paved the way. Colonel Zinga, a South African, was in charge and gracious in his welcome. "My focus," he advised, "is Kivu, both North and South. The immediate area around Goma and the city itself is largely quiet these days, but ragtag militia such as the Mai Mai and remnants of those who sparked the genocide in Rwanda, now calling themselves the FDLR do still cause problems in outlying areas. We do a lot of patrolling and meeting with local leaders in an effort to keep things peaceful. But Kivu is a huge place and movement is difficult. Even so, I must admit," he said with a smile, "we are doing a credible job. However, Ituri and Haut Uele where you are going are still quite dicey. My colleague in Bunia has the current hot seat."

Philippe asked about road safety. "Unpredictable," the

soldier responded, "most of the time, no trouble, but then out of nowhere and always in the middle of nowhere, an ambush occurs usually aimed at local vehicles with robbery as the chief motive. UNPKC convoys are rarely bothered these days."

"Can we travel with UNPKC?" Philippe asked.

"Certainly, there is always a convoy of NGO vehicles, buses and trucks that tags along whenever we move. We will have a supply convoy heading north on Thursday. You will be welcome to join."

Thursday was two days away. Philippe thought one more day in Goma would be enough. He was itching to get really started. "We will be there," he thanked the colonel.

Ndomazi was roused from a light mid-morning slumber by the noisy arrival of a military land rover. It screeched to a stop just in front of his house. An impeccably uniformed captain descended from the passenger seat. His driver, also in a crisp uniform followed along behind as the young officer approached the house. Ndomazi stood up from his chair under the mango tree. The captain came to full attention and snapped a smart salute. "Colonel Ndomazi," he greeted, "I have an important message for you from his Excellency the Minister."

Ndomazi returned the salute, accepted the proffered envelope and welcomed the soldiers. "Thank you for your trouble. You are most welcome. Please sit and have something cool to drink." He motioned for Grace, who was eagerly looking on to bring the visitors something to quench their thirst.

Ndomazi carefully opened the big brown envelope replete with Ministry of National Defense logos on the front. Inside were two smaller envelopes, one with Democratic Republic of the Congo stamps on it. He opened the other first. Marked "from the office of the minister" it was a personal note from Jean Mbaito. Years before Ndomazi had been instrumental in an odd coup d'etat that ousted dictator Bassia and replaced him with a more benevolent regime. Mbaito, under the *nom de guerre* of "the Pilot" was the chief instigator of the political change and as a result ended up as minister of defense. It was he who had inducted Ndomazi into the army and given him the rank of colonel. Ndomazi had served well and found his niche as a trainer focused especially on bush craft, his original métier.

Mbaito's note: "Cher Ami, I was very surprised to get the enclosed letter from Philippe Darman, whom we thought was dead. Life is strange. Anyway, he appears to be alive and well. He solicits your aid in a venture in northern Congo. I sent a letter back to his Kinshasa sending address to congratulate him for living and to chastise him for not telling us so. Regards, Jean."

There were two letters in the stamped envelope. The first addressed to Mbaito contained greetings and a request that the second be passed to Ndomazi. The second to Ndomazi explained Philippe's new undertaking in the Congo and requested that he join the effort. "You are by far the best tracker and most knowledgeable game expert that I know. Your help would be enormously useful as we seek to protect Garamba Park. If you choose to come, you will find me at Park Headquarters between Dungu and Faradje."

Ndomazi wanted to be extra certain that he understood the request, so he took the missive inside and had Grace, who had good French and more schooling, read it aloud to him. It was indeed an intriguing offer. He would think it over. Returning to the delivery team, Ndomazi thanked them for bringing the message and asked that they confirm back though channels that he had received the package.

Just after dawn a makeshift collection of vehicles began to line up on Avenue de la Revolution outside UNPKC headquarters waiting to join the convoy north. Philippe struck up a conversation with two French women sitting in a MSF marked Toyota Land Cruiser. They were headed for Bunia to work out of the clinic there. Liselle, a long-term Congo hand, was delighted to learn that Philippe was going to Garamba near Dungu. "You will surely meet Marie in Dungu. She is a marvel. She knows Congo better than all the rest of us and she always chooses the hardest assignment."

Shortly, led by a Toyota with flashing blue police lights on top, the convoy of about six UN trucks carrying peace keeping forces and cargo pulled out of the headquarters. The hangers-on scrambled for their vehicles and the trek began.

The convoy navigated the city streets which was not difficult in the early morning. Past the airport, mounds of busted pieces of black lava rock pushed to the shoulders showed where the road had been bulldozed open after this or that volcanic eruption. Mt. Nyamuragira loomed ahead, but only puffs of smoke indicated its internal fires. The convoy swung northwards over the shoulder between Nyamuragira and Nyirangongo both volcanoes providing evidence of the splintering of Africa along the western section of the Great Rift Valley. In the forest canopies that overhung the road, Philippe knew it was not far to the home range of the

Mountain Gorillas in the Virunga Mountains to the east. He teased Christopher about keeping a careful eye out for massive gorillas on the road. Several roadblocks encountered along this stretch remained open for all vehicles trailing the UNPKC lead car. "Thank goodness for that," Philippe thought.

The road descended to the vast Virunga plains. This area remained part of a national park and herds of antelopes, cob and waterbuck were easily seen, but elephants, rhinos, lions and buffalo were not spotted. Philippe knew that Virunga along with Queen Elizabeth in neighboring Uganda had once carried the largest biomass of any park in the world. It was sad to note the decimation that years of violence and war had wreaked on the once magnificent park. "Given time and protection," Philippe told Christopher, "the animals could flourish again." Philippe began to doubt his own words as they passed Rwindi, once park headquarters with a luxurious tourist lodge. It was abandoned and derelict, more mute evidence of the paroxysms of violence that had visited the region.

Slogging slowly through mud holes, the convoy rolled towards the looming thousand-foot-high western wall of the rift valley. The route climbed the western rift, in and out of forests, with fleeting but magnificent views of the plains below. Once out of the park, homesteads and villages appeared along the roadside. Occasionally, fruit or vegetables were lined up for sale with a hopeful merchant standing ready, but many of the habitations appeared to be empty.

Two of the UN trucks swung off at Butembo in order to rotate peacekeeping forces. Philippe surmised that the outgoing forces would be collected when the convoy returned in a day or two. It was a long drive and Philippe nodded off. He awoke as they entered Beni, the overnight stop. There was not much to the town, but the little hotel was used to accommodating transiting NGO personnel. It was satisfactory. Beer was chilled and chicken stew quite edible. Philippe chatted up the two French ladies. The two were both nurses and had spent some time in refugee camps near Goma. They talked a bit about Africa. Philippe was always impressed with folks like them. They had a strong sense of adventure, but were truly motivated by doing good, by contributing something to those in need. Shifting to other topics the three reminisced about places they all knew in Provence. That was a pleasant diversion from the reality of the war zone of North Kivu.

In the morning a smaller convoy regrouped. It would be a day's drive to Bunia - more bad roads, still with the possibility of ambush. Fortunately, several of the UN vehicles were going to Bunia, so the escort remained. The road was again mostly through forested regions. They were now on the eastern edge of the great Congo basin, the second largest rainforest - after the Amazon - in the world. Yet Philippe caught glances of the mountain wall of the Ruwenzoris to the east. Although clouds forever hid the summits, it was difficult to phantom right there on the equator that the peaks were clad in snowy glaciers. Philippe remembered that Ptolemy somehow had heard of these peaks thousands of years ago and dubbed the chain the Mountains of the Moon. They were reputed to be the source of the Nile. Indeed, all the streams on the eastern slopes did flow eventually into the Nile

At the junction of the Bunia-Kisangani road, the convoy halted. The dozen private trucks headed west towards Kisangani, some 300 miles away, would henceforth be on their own. Philippe wished them God speed. He knew that he and Christopher would be on their own before long as well without even the comfort of other vehicles. The rest of the convoy turned east towards Bunia, only about sixty hard miles distant. In Bunia Philippe bid adieu to the two French nurses as they veered off towards the MSF compound. The ECP team checked into a respectable hotel. They made a round of contact with UNPKC officials, H.R. Patel's cousin and the local office of the Ministry for Wildlife and Tourism. The Moroccan Major at UNPKC confirmed that the UN had withdrawn troops from Dungu because the situation there had settled down nicely after the Lord's Resistance Army was chased out of the region by the U.S./Ugandan force. He carefully advised that although the U.S./Ugandan force had publicly left the Congo, Philippe should not be surprised if clandestine residual operations occurred from time to time. The major said his men would do a road patrol regularly from Bunia to Faradje, Dungu, Isiro and back, so folks at Garamba could count on periodic visits. Philippe welcomed that confirmation and invited the patrols to pause overnight at Garamba Park headquarters.

As he and Christopher took dinner - a stringy roasted chicken with fried potatoes - in the hotel restaurant, Philippe remarked, "At last all the preliminaries are over. Now we get to do our job. Christopher, there is still time to opt out. If you want, you can return to Kinshasa from here. No hard feelings on my part."

Christopher smiled, "No, No. I signed up to be an elephant man, but still have not even seen an elephant. I am with you. It has been a great adventure for me even just this far. I want to keep going."

"Great," Philippe responded, "I hoped you felt that way. Tomorrow we are off to Garamba." They clinked beers.

A fter a quick breakfast, Christopher carefully checked the
Toyota. Tires were good, oil full, gas tank full, plus two
five-gallon jerry cans. She was ready to go. Philippe slipped
into the left-hand passenger seat. He quickly loaded a clip into
an AK-47. "Best to be prepared," he quipped. Christopher
nodded solemnly, not sure of what might ensue.

The road north was bad, one track. Rutted mud holes
alternated with sandy washes. The terrain, however, was
no longer forest, but scattered woodland verging into open
savannah. The homesteads, farms and villages on the
outskirts of Bunia gave way to more openness, not unlike
the terrain Philippe remembered around his hunting camp
east of Bria. They passed a slow moving, smoke spewing
country bus jammed to capacity and with an incredibly high
load, including two goats, tied on the roof. The bus swayed
precariously as it tilted back and forth but stayed upright.
"However crowded," Philippe commented, "It is good to see
normal commerce underway."

Although Philippe knew that the tribal conflagrations
that troubled Ituri Province were less prevalent the further
north they travelled, he remained alert. Several hours into
the journey, Christopher slowed seeing a log across the road.
Philippe tensed. "Be alert," he cautioned. Sure enough, as the
Toyota slowed, two men sauntered out from under a nearby
tree. One approached Philippe's window.

"*Bonjour, patron,*" he greeted. "*Il faut payer passage.*"

"*Non,*" Philippe responded. "We are government officials en route to Garamba Park. No payments from us." He raised the AK as he spoke.

Seeing Philippe's gun. The man quickly backed away. "*Oui, Oui, patron, continuez.*"

Christopher quickly maneuvered around the log and drove on. "Good work, patron," he said with relief.

"It was just a shakedown," Philippe retorted. "We could have paid, but best to have made a statement. They will remember our vehicle and Garamba and will be leery of any confrontation in the future." He settled back as they bounced along.

Sometime later Christopher queried, "Patron, can I ask a question?"

"Sure," Philippe replied, "What's on your mind?"

"Well," Christopher continued, "I will become an elephant man because it is new to me and an opportunity to advance, but why do you come to this forgotten corner of the Congo?"

Philippe ruminated a minute. "You know I was a professional hunter in the Central African Republic for fifteen years. I found that I loved the bush. There I was completely responsible for myself and for those in my charge. I loved being on foot in the wild areas. It was never quiet. The wind whistled softly through the leaves, birds twittered, insects buzzed and darted around, little creatures scurried about. The sun often hung heavy above and the smells - of flowers, trees, dust, carrion, dung, rain or mud assaulted my senses. I've missed that." He paused. "I also headed a small community. My workers, their wives and children depended on me...and I on them. I've missed that responsibility as well.

"I abandoned all of that after a run-in with poachers and thieves; men who killed the woman I loved. It took me years to settle my mind. Then this opportunity came along. So, to answer your question, I reckon I am doing this to soothe my soul, to regain a balance I've lost. A balance I think I can find again at Garamba.... we'll see."

Before long they entered Faradje, a small town of several thousand residents. It was essentially only a crossroads for commercial purposes - a couple of meagerly stocked stores, no petrol station, a forlorn market where dozens of makeshift stands stood empty (it was not market day), no hotels and no restaurants, only a few bars. "Ugh," Philippe thought, out loud he said, "this is one of our closest towns, but it doesn't look as if it will be much use." Christopher nodded in agreement. He had seen many little beleaguered towns in his native Kongo Province, but nothing as dry, dusty and neglected as Faradje.

Beyond Faradje, the road deteriorated even more. It was about thirty miles to Garamba Park Headquarters, but the park itself began just outside the town. Consequently, there were no villages, houses or fields. Head high green/yellow grass encroached on the one lane track from both sides. In places it was like driving down a tunnel. While Christopher concentrated on driving, Philippe carefully studied the terrain looking for evidence of both animal and human presence. He saw little.

Christopher stopped at a half-tilted signpost indicating Garamba Park Office with an arrow. "So here we are," he stated.

Philippe agreed, smiled and got out. "We might as well start with straightening the sign." He pushed it back upright and stacked several rocks around it to ensure stability. The smell of the dry bush laced with a tinge of herbal scents invigorated him bringing back flashes of his previous life. "I feel home," he rejoiced laughing. The pressures of the last month slipped away. Christopher joined in. "Come on," Philippe urged, "let's go make you an elephant man!"

The Toyota bumped slowly along the track. Soon a cluster of buildings came into view. Christopher pulled to a halt before the biggest one. As the dust settled, Philippe opened the door. A line of six men stood at full attention. Their sergeant greeted Philippe, *"Monsieur le directeur, les guards de chasse de la parc de Garamba, vous accueillent."* They presented arms with old AK47s.

Philippe acknowledged the welcome. "Thank you very much for your greeting. I am indeed quite pleased to be here, and I look forward to working closely with you all." He ordered them to stand at ease and, starting with the sergeant, shook hands with each man.

Sergeant Elijah Malulu showed them around. The camp showed its age and years of neglect. Elijah noted that the director's house had been freshly cleaned in anticipation of Philippe's arrival. The park had received word about a week earlier over the sporadically functioning short wave radio. His men had been listening for an arriving vehicle ever since. The park office was rudimentary - several desks and chairs, an old map of the park tacked on the wall. Once the compound had electricity, but the generator gave up the ghost many years earlier. Elijah sadly advised that the generator had also run the pump, so there was no piped water either. Fortunately, the river was only a kilometer distant, an easy walk for the women. In addition to the office and the director's house there was a *maison de passage* for visitors, a workshop and storehouse. The rangers lived in a separate little village cluster of small cement block houses which were surrounded by a dozen or so mud houses of traditional construction.

"Well," Philippe said to Elijah and Christopher, "I did not expect much and that is about what we got. Even so we can make do." They set about moving in. Philippe took the director's house, Christopher one of the rooms in the *maison de passage*. They set up solar panels for the office and connected the computers and charging stations for the satellite phone. As a test, Philippe rang up Jan Owens at the Elephant Conservation Project office in Kinshasa. It was a decent connection. "Jan, Philippe here. We are at Garamba, getting settled in and ready to work." They chatted about the travel, established a time for a regular weekly call. Owens wished them well.

Elijah proved to be a wealth of knowledge about the park. He had been serving as a ranger there for nearly twenty years. The rest of the men too had family origins in the region and had been in service for years. Elijah complained that pay had been erratic, especially the last few years. He hoped that with a new director that situation would improve. Philippe assured him that it would.

Garamba was a vast expanse of land, 80 miles on a side. It was mostly acacia grassland, i.e. fairly open grassland with bushes and trees scattered throughout. The park was bordered on the north by the Mbomu river that constituted the international boundary with South Sudan. Several other good-sized streams flowed through the park. There were gentle hills and valleys and a low steeper range of hills to the west. In the wet season grass often rose to the height of three meters making patrolling difficult. The combination of adequate water and lots of herbage rendered Garamba a haven for Africa's big game. The Park once harbored perhaps 20,000 elephants, hundreds of white rhinos, thousands of hippos, cape buffaloes and giraffes as well as tens of thousands of cob, other antelope and colorful birds. However, due to war and poaching, especially the predations of the Lords' Resistance Army, the numbers of big game had precipitously declined. Rhinos were gone, giraffes down to about a hundred and elephants cut in half, if not more.

Elijah said the western reaches of the park led into Wayamba territory, a proud, sometimes fierce and very isolated tribal group. He said that rangers stayed out of their lands and in turn the Wayamba generally respected park boundaries. They were not poachers. Poachers generally came from Sudan. They had targeted the docile rhino for their horns and the elephants for their tusks. Most of the contraband was taken back to Sudan. Although poaching began small it bloomed into bigger business with the advent of trucks and markets. During the ten years or so that the Lords' Resistance Army was in the area, poaching by them with automatic weapons became even more widespread. Additionally, LRA fighters purposely attacked villages and homesteads, killing, kidnapping children, pillaging and sowing terror.

In their attack on park headquarters five years earlier, they killed seven - two rangers and their families. The then director was shot, but lived, but then left. There had been no director since. He added that he and all the surviving staff had fled into the park when the first shots were fired. They hid for two days before returning. They found headquarters buildings ransacked. What food there was, was taken. The raiders wanted trucks, but fearing an attack, Park staff earlier took wheels and batteries and buried them in the bush. Philippe applauded this cleverness. Elijah accepted congratulations with aplomb. He said the land rover, the truck and the tractor were back together, but needed new batteries and fuel.

Elijah confirmed that twelve rangers were currently assigned to the Park. Six were on patrol by foot to the north and should return within the next few days. Without vehicles, Elijah noted, not much territory could be covered.

Asked if LRA remnants remained in the area, Elijah said no. For several years American and Ugandan troops along with a contingent from the Congolese Army operated in the north along the river. In fact, they established a base camp there and had many helicopters coming in and out. Apparently, the foreign armies did not effectively engage the LRA in firefights. Rather than fight, LRA personnel just slipped away, but the presence and the pressure did chase the LRA out of the park, mostly out of Congo and much further west into the CAR and further north in South Sudan. One advantage of the foreign military presence was that it did deter poaching, but by then a lot of damage had already been done. With those troops now gone, poachers again felt emboldened and park resources to combat them were meager.

As part of an initial orientation, Philippe wanted to see some elephants. Plus, he wanted Christopher to meet some as well. Early the next morning Elijah guided them to a river about ten miles from camp. "They like this spot," he counseled, "and will come to drink about mid-morning." The team waited patiently concealed on a bank overlooking the river shallows.

Soon there was movement in the brush and slight noise of big creatures accompanied by a low rumbling that the men felt as much as heard. A large cow suddenly appeared in the clearing above the river. She stood still raised her trunk in the air, sampling the wind. She flapped her ears as she carefully looked around. Apparently satisfied that all was okay, she lowered her trunk. About then three juveniles broke from the bush and rushed joyfully into the river. They splashed and cavorted about as the rest of the group came down to drink. It was quite noisy with squeaks and squeals of the youngsters backed up with harrumphs and grunts from the adults. Christopher counted seventeen elephants in all. The leader, an old cow - Christopher would learn to dub her the matriarch - took her turn drinking and spraying water over her back, but she remained wary, always on guard. The others, however, especially the youngsters frolicked in the water, chasing each other around and rolling in the mud. A mother with a very small infant carefully eased the baby into the water, caressing it with her trunk. For its part the baby stuck close to mom, even underneath her when possible. The baby nursed; obviously that's where breakfast was.

"Are these mostly females?" Christopher asked.

"All the adults are female," Philippe replied. "Some of the younger ones are males, but they leave the family group as adults and hang out together for a few years. Thereafter some may stay in close association with their buddies, but others are solitary. Even so the males usually stay in proximity to a family group. They are always desirous to mate. They come in to visit periodically and to test by smell whether any of the girls are ready."

Elijah said, "I know this group. Look at the matriarch's ears. See the tear about halfway up in the left ear and the notch near the top on the right one. That plus tusk configuration and overall size, even back shape helps tell them apart. This old lady has been bossing this family around for years. As a family group they have stayed closer to park headquarters than others and have not yet been savaged by poachers.

"Look over there," he pointed. "A bull is paying a visit." An obviously larger individual sauntered down the far bank and waded across the shallow stream. The matriarch fixed on him but made no move to challenge him. "She knows him," Elijah commented. "Maybe even one of her sons." The bull drank by sucking water into his truck then sticking it into his mouth. He sprayed himself with water, had a good roll in the shallows, then stopped to greet several of the herd by touching trunks. He seemed content to just hang around.

"He has bigger tusks to go with his size. I recognize this one too. He roams more widely than the family group. It is good to see him back in this area. Poachers prefer the big bulls obviously because their ivory is bigger, but they are harder to find whereas family herds are relatively easy to track."

The men sat for another half hour watching the elephants go about their ablutions. Finally, the matriarch signaled it was time to go and the elephants dutifully followed her back into the bush.

"They will feed for several hours," Philippe told Christopher, "then doze and rest during the heat of the day, before coming back for water about dusk."

Driving back to headquarters, Phillipe asked, "so, Christopher, what do you think?"

"Awesome, I never thought they would be such a family and so attentive to each other. I am going to like being an elephant man. What do I do next?"

"We'll go over some census charts the Project sent out with us. You will have to learn how to fill them in correctly. For the census we'll need numbers, genders, ages and territories. This will mean you will have to spend lots of time in the bush." Christopher nodded affirmatively.

"Elijah, who is your best elephant tracker?"

"That would be Toma. He is one of those out on patrol."

"Great, we can assign him and Christopher to the elephant census team. Over the next few months, we must get a good count of the remaining population."

Ndomazi carefully disassembled the rifle. He snuggly wrapped the parts and tucked them into his duffle. He embraced his wife and gave her a wad of cash. "I might be gone several months. Garamba Park in the Congo is my destination. I will probably be able to get word back to you at some point. I taught Grace about the bank in Bambari, so she can get more money if you need it."

Shouldering his duffle, Ndomazi boarded the local bus for Bambari, there he changed to a bus headed for Bangassou and the border. He was careful to travel as incognito as possible. He wore old clothes and flip flops. His boots and better attire packed away. He did not want his rifle to be seized. He was only slightly worried about Congolese border officials. There was a good bit of local traffic across the river ferry, but officials focused on market mamas, obvious businessmen and especially foreign over-landers, if any should be voyaging that day. Ndomazi was a small nondescript elder who did not attract attention.

Bus travel, as always, was crowded and slow. Congolese buses were even more decrepit than their Central African counterparts. Fortunately, there were no breakdowns. Ndomazi had to stay the night in Buta but continued on to Isiro and Dungu the next day. After having circled down into the Congo basin rainforest, Ndomazi was pleased to be back into the bush filled savannah he was so accustomed to. Hitching a ride into the park took time, but eventually a truck came along. Ndomazi negotiated a fare and climbed on. Disembarking at the now erect signpost, he walked the last few miles to headquarters.

"We have a visitor," Christopher nodded at the small figure trudging up the road.

"My God," Philippe exclaimed, "It's him." He rushed out to greet his friend. With back slaps and huge grins all around, Philippe welcomed Ndomazi to Garamba. Telling Christopher, Elijah and rangers who gathered around, "Meet Colonel Ndomazi, the greatest bushman and tracker in Africa. He is on loan to the Congo and will be of great assistance to us in improving our anti-poaching operations."

Later, Ndomazi chuckled, "I bring greetings from "the pilot." He and the rest of us thought you were dead. You surprised us. I last saw you crawling onto that cargo plane carrying the tusks."

Philippe summed up succinctly, "Yes, I was on that plane, it crashed in the deep forest. I was the only survivor. Jill and the pilots died in the crash. I was saved by a pygmy band and healed of my injuries. Ultimately, I made it back to France and then on to the Caribbean. After some years there I got bored and so found this assignment."

Changing the topic, "After making it to France I read how Jean managed the rebellion that ousted Bassia. I know that you were his right-hand man in that venture."

"True," the old gent replied, "I helped him organize fighters, plan and execute operations, but it wasn't really very difficult. Bassia's regime crumbled. Mbaito and friends have done a good job since. He set me up as a trainer and advisor in the army. I did that for a while, but it was too much hustle and bustle. I missed the quiet of the bush. I retired to my village, but your letter piqued my interest. Maybe I too still have something useful to do."

Smiling craftily Ndomazi said, "I brought you something." Reaching into his duffle he pulled out the still well wrapped rifle.

Philippe whistled in admiration, "My Weatherly." They assembled the weapon. It was in immaculate condition. Philippe shouldered it and aimed out the window. "It feels great, just as it should, but it's no longer mine. She's yours. You preserved her, you kept her. She's yours. She will stand you in good stead here in Garamba." Ndomazi nodded appreciatively at confirmation of the gift.

During their weekly teleconference Jan Owens said, "something very interesting here yesterday. The journalist I pointed to the ivory smuggling story produced...and it is quite something. It has certainly stirred the pot. I emailed you the story."

Murder Tied to Smuggling Ring. The Daily Post investigative team has discovered that the gruesome murder of Marcel Ntumbwa 22 of Nagliema neighborhood was tied to his personal quest of outlining the elements of an ivory smuggling ring. Ntumbwa was found dead in his abode about midnight on June 14. According to the police report he had been strangled by a wire. In a bizarre development Ntumbwa's tongue was cut out, apparently because he was seen as an informer betraying the smugglers. Reportedly Ntumbwa was getting ready to expose the criminals. Ntumbwa was employed by Best African Hardwoods, a Chinese owned firm that exports timber to Asia. Reliable sources advise that the export company is suspected of illegally exporting ivory, which is unlawful in Congo and equally forbidden by international treaties. A representative of Mme Ching, the owner of Best African Hardwoods, declined to comment on the death of their employee or the allegation of smuggling. The Daily Post has to ask, who else is involved in the destruction of Congo's national heritage?

Philippe posted back. "Thanks for the update. Although I don't yet have much information about poaching routes, rangers here assert that ivory from Garamba moves north and east through South Sudan. We should know more in time. By the way, Christopher is working out fine. Ciao."

At the U.S. embassy, Economic Counselor Eric Strom stood looking out of his third story window to the street below. The *Avenue des Aviators* was crowded as usual with people jostling along the sidewalks and vehicles jamming the street. He was mulling over the item about smuggling in the morning paper. Returning to his desk he rang up the USAID officer who should know more about it.

"Bill. Eric here, I am looking at the news bit about ivory smuggling, what more do you know?"

"Well. It is true as far as it goes. Best African Hardwoods has been fingered as a smuggler for some time. We have gone as far to insist that at least one cargo destined for Taipei be inspected upon arrival for contraband, specially tusks. That should happen next week. If ivory is found, we will use that fact to vociferously complain here in Congo. A private contact confided that there is a group of customs authorities, led by the deputy director, that is implicated in the smuggling. This should be enough to have him removed, others sacked as well and will certainly be adequate to get Mme. Ching expelled."

Eric responded, "I trust you're right. Corruption is rife in Kinshasa but is usually conducted in quiet with heads turned away. A public brouhaha will compel action. Those who are caught red-handed suffer and others just keep a lower profile. How can we keep the heat on 'til we hear back from China?"

He paused, "let's sit down with our public affairs folks. An article here or there plus some save-the-wildlife stuff on Facebook won't hurt. What do you think?"

"I'm in, I'll phone Paula and set up a meeting. Is later this morning okay?

hristopher and Toma sat down together and elaborated a schedule to track elephant families. They carefully went over the census sheets, so they would know what to report. Ndomazi and Elijah outlined a program for ranger training. Philippe advised that he was especially keen that the rangers learn to shoot. Recognizing that he needed mobility to get these various jobs done, Philippe made a list and organized a visit to Dungu to purchase fuel and batteries in order to get the park vehicles back in operation. After loading a fifty-gallon drum into the Toyota, Elijah asked if some of the wives could go along. Philippe readily agreed. Shortly seven women in colorful go-to-town garb accompanied by two infants on backs, crowded into the vehicle. None of the women spoke French, but they chattered happily in Azande. Philippe concentrated on the road.

Upon arrival near the central market, Philippe gave each woman 1000 Congolese francs - about three dollars. Delighted, they volubly expressed appreciation, "merci, merci, patron!" Philippe pointed at the sun, moved his point down towards the horizon and conveyed his message that they were to reassemble at this point about four o'clock. The women nodded understanding. Philippe briefly thought to himself that parceling out 1000 francs set a bad precedent, but immediately dismissed the idea. He could handle twenty dollars or so every now and then and it was great for morale.

Philippe went to call on M.R. Patel, a cousin, of course, of the eastern Congo Patels. Money transfer arrangements were in place, so Philippe drew a large sum. He purchased diesel, appropriate batteries and other items from the list. Deciding he needed more information about who was who and what was up in Dungu, he decided to call on Marie, the doctor with *Medecins Sans Frontieres*. At the hospital, he a white visitor, was greeted cautiously. But when he asked for Dr. Marie he was met with smiles. An orderly was sent to fetch her. Soon a slim, brown haired woman dressed in hospital scrubs approached. She had a busy look on her face. With a steely stare she looked him up and down. "I don't believe we've met."

Caught off balance, Philippe stammered, "I am Philippe Darman, the newly appointed director of Garamba Park. I met several of your colleagues, Lizelle and Michelle, on travels north from Goma to Bunia. They insisted that I contact you when in Dungu. So... here I am."

"Ah, I see. I do remember mention of you. Welcome to this poor little corner of the world. What can I do for you?"

"Well, clearly I am new. I wonder if you might share your knowledge of who is who in this town and what the issues are. Can I invite you to lunch?"

She checked her watch. "Indeed, it is about that time. And yes, I could probably vent. So, let's do it. Give me a minute."

Marie returned quickly having shed her hospital cloak. She suggested a little place nearby that usually had decent samosas, edible chicken and chilled Fanta orange sodas. Shrugging her shoulders, she said there was not much else.

Marie proved to be a talker. She quickly relaxed in Philippe's company and shared her knowledge. She said the deputy governor was a cipher, but often not present. She thought highly of the police chief. He had good sense and seemed focused on doing the job properly. She did not really have a good measure of the new army commander. His predecessor had been okay, although somewhat heavy handed in dealing with displaced persons. She confided that she had come to Dungu in the aftermath of the wave of displacements caused by the Lords' Resistance Army some years ago. That crisis caused MSF and other NGOs associated with UN relief efforts to set up shop in Dungu. Ultimately almost twenty thousand persons fled for safety to Dungu. UNPKC made the town a headquarters and provided security for the camps and the NGO workers. However, as the LRA was chased out of the region by the American/Ugandan/Congolese military operation, the people slowly drifted back home. The last ones were forcibly moved out of the camps by the army. So, the camps closed. NGO money dried up and even UNPKC contingents left. MSF too pulled out camp staff, but by then Marie was already working mostly out of the hospital. She made a compelling case to stay and MSF acquiesced. She concluded, "that's my story."

Asked how bad the LRA was, Marie scrunched up her brow. "They added horrible on top of terrible. Congo is poor and folks suffer from all sorts of maladies - malaria, measles, TB, malnutrition, even Ebola from time to time in this region. Life is especially harsh for pregnant women. They don't eat properly because they cannot, they work in the fields until the last moment, and few have any prenatal care. Women do not get much respect. Most men think of them as chattel. Although customs vary, many are essentially sold as brides in their teenage years. Like all societies, Congo has domestic violence, but the LRA brought a new viciousness of sexual violence. The men they confronted were summarily killed, but the women from prepubescent girls upward were raped, often repeatedly. By the time they got to me, survivors were damaged physically, but often I could help with that. The trauma, however, went into realms of fear and culture that were beyond my competence. Yet, we tried. No real psychological expertise was available, but survivors' groups in safe places let the women share and comfort one another. Slowly the immediate impact was passed, yet I know that memories have scarred them for life.

"A lingering problem of rape is unwanted babies. Unsanctioned children are a problem for families. Usually the mother will conclude that its origins were not the child's fault, so will love and accept it. The mother's family may do so as well. Occasionally, the mother or the family will totally reject the child. In those cases, it is shuttled off to another caregiver or an orphanage. But whatever the circumstances, the child, the mother and the family, bear a stigma. The child will always remind its elders of the circumstances of its conception. It is a stigma that the child will carry throughout life. It may always be considered on a lower rung, denied education, forced to labor or beg. The children of violence in this part of Congo are not yet adolescents, so it is too early to tell what all of the social ramifications will be."

She paused... then continued, "that is all history. Today I am back dealing with everyday trauma, mostly troublesome pregnancies and very sick children. It is quite distressing to think of those issues as normal."

Philippe could only nod. Marie said, "enough about me what is your program?"

"To be concise I intend to get the park on its feet, especially to control - hopefully halt - poaching. I am also charged with counting the big game, particularly elephants, in order to find out what there really is to save. Given meager resources to start, it will be a challenge, but if we register success, I think the big wildlife NGOs will provide additional monies."

"Good luck with that." The conversation returned to Dungu. Queries about Patel's reliability, best market stalls, problematic delivery of medical supplies, and the complete absence of French government assistance projects in eastern Congo. In parting Marie said, "whenever you're in Dungu, drop by. I've enjoyed our talk and would appreciate updates of your progress."

After lunch Philippe called on the chief of police. He reviewed his anti-poaching mandate and sought assurances that any poachers turned over to the police would be suitably charged and punished. The chief asserted that would indeed be the case. Next was the market. Philippe loaded up on pineapples, mangoes, bananas, tomatoes, onions and all the scrawny little potatoes he could find. A stop by the butcher's provided a hunk of stringy beef. Philippe lamented that as a park officer he could no longer hunt for the pot, so the butcher's fare would have to do.

The ladies were waiting at the appointed hour and spot. Like Philippe they had bags of foodstuffs, plus several live chickens and other goods to be stacked into the Toyota. Evidently everyone had a successful day.

With a little work the park's vehicles were soon functional. Philippe breathed a sigh of relief, now he could bear down on the poaching problem. But first he wanted to ensure that the rangers were up to a more vigorous interdiction program. He knew it was inevitable that shooting would be necessary. Solid training and discipline would be crucial to success. The training that Ndomazi was supervising went well. Convincing the rangers to fire single shots aimed at a specific target rather than a helter-skelter spray was key to making them marksmen. Gradually they became more proficient. Ndomazi also taught small unit tactics - how to surround a target group, how to move in surreptitiously, how to choose ground and how to ensure a safe exit path. Ndomazi said that the rangers were already accomplished in bush arts. They could identify most prints and knew how to use the wind. Several, including Toma were excellent trackers. "Like me," he praised, "Toma just senses where the animal will go."

"Great," Philippe exclaimed. "Next week, we'll go north and scout along the river. I also want to see what is left of the military camp the Americans left behind." Meanwhile, Philippe sent the elephant census team out every morning. Their list of groups - they decided to categorize them alphabetically - was up to "F". Roving males bore numbers beginning with "1".

Taking three vehicles - the Toyota, the Land Rover and

the Tata truck - the park team headed north. It was slow going, but the track was viable. Mud holes had mostly dried up and stream crossing were easily fordable by the four-wheel drive vehicles. The pace of movement gave Philippe time to more fully assess the terrain - the flora, fauna and geography. Once they spotted elephants in the distance, so the elephant team spun off for a look-see. Elsewhere, there was a group of giraffes grazing amongst the treetops along a watercourse. Giraffe too were targeted by poachers. Philippe remembered that in the Central African Republic, Chadian horsemen would ride down on a giraffe, kill it and only take the tail as a memento of their prowess. Antelope scattered about in small herds or singly paused to stare at the trucks before dashing off. Occasionally a wart hog family with tails held high trotted hurriedly across the track. A rumble of hooves pounding the ground and cloud of dust indicated a herd of cape buffalo spooked by the convoy's approach. Bird life was prolific. Weavers burdened selected acacia trees with hundreds of hanging nests. Vultures circled in the distant sky. Small colorful songbirds darted in and out of trees and bushes. Every so often a gorgeous lilac breasted roller perched on a bush alongside the track. Although the team saw no lions, Philippe was assured that they too called the park home. All things considered, Garamba still seemed to have all the necessary basics for a viable park - everything except rhinoceros. Even so, if park rangers could protect what was there and stabilize the big game populations, there was hope they would expand.

An hour or so before dark the little convoy rolled into an obviously man-made opening. "This was the military camp," Elijah explained. There was not much left. Rolls of concertina wire along a falling down fence was about it.

There was evidence of how the camp was laid out with tent platforms in a line, but no platforms or tents were left. There was some debris scattered about. Some broken solar panels, a derelict generator, busted tanks and pipes and wires leading to what was clearly a 6" wide well head. Philippe inspected that. He thought there was still a pump down inside. Without electricity there would be no water. Elijah said that folks from the nearby village, a few miles outside the park boundary had been told to help themselves. "Obviously, they did," Philippe observed. Despite the abandoned feel of the place, it was a good site. It was situated on a rise so as to catch the breeze. The park team set up camp.

First thing the next morning Philippe, Elijah and two rangers visited the nearby village. They summoned the elders to a palaver. The old men knew Elijah and welcomed him warmly. With Elijah interpreting, Philippe introduced himself as the new park director. His mission was to halt poaching, especially the taking of elephants for their tusks. The government empowered him as director to use force in order to deter poaching. Not only would poachers be arrested and imprisoned, but if they resisted arrest they might be shot. Philippe asked that the elders convey this warning to surrounding communities, especially those across the river in South Sudan. He added that Garamba Park was a tremendous resource not just for the Congo but for the wider world. When poaching and violence were constrained in northern Congo, then tourists would arrive. Their visiting would rebound in benefits, especially jobs, for communities surrounding the park.

The elders listened attentively. In turn they welcomed renewed attention to the park and to their village. They pledged that no one from the village poached elephants, that was done, they averred, by raiding parties from Sudan and by the LRA. The men complained of no school for their grandchildren and no access to health care. One of the old men said, "we are troubled for our youth. There is little for them here, only traditional life of farming and hunting. Young people seek more. They want school, fancy clothes, bicycles, motos, and cell phones. Often, they leave. One boy who went to Bunia, fell in with a bandit group. His family heard bad reports. Finally, an uncle found him and urged him to come home. He refused and berated his elder. The boy said, 'my gun is my family now. It is my father and my mother. It is everything to me. I will not give it up.'" The old man paused, "What are we to do?"

There was more discussion of the isolation of the village and problems of linkage to the outside world. Philippe listened. The elders saw him as a representative of government, and they asked Philippe to address their many grievances. Philippe assured them that he heard their message. The meeting ended amicably.

Afterwards, Philippe told Elijah, "we have laid down a marker on poaching. At minimum folks along the border here will be warned that we mean business."

Upon returning to camp, they found two rangers guarding a couple seated under a shade tree. Elijah investigated. He then told Philippe that the man did not speak much Azande, but appeared to be Ugandan, maybe a member of the Lords' Resistance Army. Intrigued Philippe went to check it out. As Philippe approached the man in question rose to attention, saluted and said in good English, "Sir! Godfrey Owino here, Sir!" Philippe returned the salute. He regarded the man. Probably mid-twenties, skinny as a rail, not tall but broad shouldered, wiry with ropy muscles on his dark arms. His facial features, widely spaced eyes and a flat nose, plus two missing lower teeth, indicated his differences from the Azande rangers. He was dressed in rags, worn out pants, a torn shirt and badly abused combat boots. The woman with him - Philippe saw she had an infant on her back - also looked worn and weary.

"So, who are you and why are you here?" Philippe queried.

"My story, Sir, is that I escaped from the Lords' Resistance Army. My wife Sia and I have hidden and wandered for years, mostly shunned by villagers we contacted. They feared me because I was once LRA or they feared that LRA men would come for me and attack them. Sometimes someone would help, but eventually we were forced out. I can never go home to Uganda, but we are trying to get back to her people the Wayamba who live near here."

"You know that this area is a national park?"

"Yes, Sir. I know. I know it well. I was a LRA fighter in this region for years. I have poached in the park, even helped kill a rhino. I know all the river crossings, the game trails and the interior water holes. It was in this park or maybe just outside it that Sia was taken and when my life began to change."

"Tell me more. How did it start? How did you join the LRA?"

"Sir, I was fourteen and had just entered first form at St. Anselm's Boys Secondary School outside of Kitgum. Kony's men came in the night. It was dark. There was much shooting. The watchmen, old men armed with only a torch and clubs, were killed. The LRA men - many were only boys my size or smaller -invaded my dormitory. There was lots of screaming and shouting. They had guns and clubs. They beat us. One my friends had his skull cracked open and his brains leaked out onto the floor. Soon they lined us up, tied together and forced us to run away with them. It terrifying. Boys that cried or shit in their pants were summarily shot. Their bodies left on path.

"We taken to bush camp. Finally, we were given water, but nothing to eat. They starved us for days. We become very weak. We forced to move every two or three nights because the army was after us. During this time Commander Julius interrogated us about names and families. If he did not like our answers, he beat us. He found that my home village not far off. The commander's men trained us to be fighters. They showed us how to use guns. They taught that Kony like Christ. He was destined to cleanse and save the Acholi people from their sins, from cooperation with Museveni and from modern ways. The Bible, although no one had one, was our guide. To go against Kony and LRA beliefs was death. Boys that were weak were taken to the bush and never seen again. I lost three friends that way. James could not stop crying at night. One morning he gone.

"Several weeks after my capture, Commander Julius said that on General Kony's orders his men would raid my village that night. I was to come along. In short, the LRA soldiers raided the village. My family - father, mother and two sisters - captured. They were paraded before me. I told that as a new recruit for the LRA I was to sever all links with my past. I was ordered to shoot my parents. If not, we all be killed. I was trembling. How could I do this? I still remember my father's eyes as he said, "do it son, save yourself." I closed my eyes and pulled trigger. Other shots rang out. When I looked my parents lay dead. My sisters wailed. "Enjoy them," Commander Julius told his men. I stifled a moan; my youngest sister Amana was only eleven. I stumbled away.

"So, I became one of them. I became a LRA man. I became hardened to violence, to killing and to death. I operated with Commander Julius in Uganda and was compelled to stay with him when we trooped into Sudan after Uganda and Sudan made a deal that cut off support to General Kony. In this region we camped in forest just north of the river. We raided villages around here for food and for women and for a few recruits, but these people are not Acholi so doctrine of Acholiness did not apply. At some point Julius and other colonels go to Juba to negotiate peace with Museveni, we hoped they would reach a deal, I was told they did, but Kony refused to accept it. We stayed on in the bush. Every now and then someone would run away. I tried once but was caught and whipped.

"I enjoyed the bush. Hunting for wart hog or antelope was far better than raiding villages. We began to kill elephants for their ivory. The colonels had contacts to sell the tusks, same for the rhino I helped kill. We the shooters never saw money, only few bottles of whiskey every now and then. I know that LRA fighters raided the park headquarters, but I not with them. I was deep in the park. About that same time other LRA men captured four girls bathing in a stream. They brought them back to our camp. One was Sia. The girls were parceled out. As a long serving soldier, I was given her. She was to cook, care for me and provide sex. She did, but over time we become attached. I would not let anyone else touch her. We couldn't talk much at first. She had no language but Kiyamba, but we made do.

"When the Americans come the small bands of LRA were pressed to move west into CAR and north into the empty regions of eastern Sudan. Kony led us, but rarely stayed with us. He was always somewhere nearby. When I saw him, he ranted about his destiny and his blessing by the Lord. Fighters dropped out, some were captured, and others reported to the Americans. Mostly we stayed hidden and moved around a lot. By this time Sia was pregnant. She birthed a boy, but he died the next day. She was weak. I decided it was time to quit. We snuck away one night and have been moving on ever since. Later she again birthed a baby, this time the one she carries. My daughter Amana.

"We crossed the river several weeks ago and were fixing to move south, when your men found us this morning. "

Philippe probed further, specifically for Sia's story. She was quite shy, but under prodding agreed to share. Elijah translated. He said she spoke an odd version of Azande. Sia said she was of the Wayamba people and had never ventured into the wider world. Almost no one from the tribe ever left their home village, especially girls. One day, she, a sister and two cousins walked about a mile downstream from their village to a bathing place often used by women. While there they were accosted by six or seven LRA men who sprung unexpectedly from the bush. They were kidnapped and compelled to go with the men. For hours until dark they were rushed along, beaten if they cried or complained. Finally, they came to a camp where several dozen other men were located. They were paraded around, stripped naked, prodded and poked. Finally, each girl was given to a fighter. She became the property of Godfrey. She said he took her that night. It was her first time and was quite painful, but he did not hit her. Over the next weeks and months, she lived in fear. Fear that it would get worse coupled with hope that somehow, she could get away. That opportunity never came. Shortly the band moved across the river into Sudan and then again and again. She had no idea where she was. Godfrey, however, guarded her. He even fought a colleague once who wanted her for sex. He said she was his alone. She was glad for that small bit of security. Ultimately, she made her peace with the situation and began to think of Godfrey as a husband, she was after all functioning fully as a wife. She hated the LRA way of life: always on the move, never a house or a garden, constant fear of attack, hiding in the undergrowth when the helicopters buzzed above, no friends or sisters. She became pregnant and had a baby that died. Then Godfrey decided to quit the LRA. She happily agreed. They snuck away in the night, hid during the day and travelled again at night for almost a week. Finally, safely away from those fanatics, they found no peace or longer-term place to stay. She had another baby. Slowly they moved back towards Congo and her home. She did not know if she could go home, especially with a non-Wayamba husband, but they saw no other options. She wanted to see her mother.

'Wow,' Philippe thought, 'what stories, what trials and tribulations. These two have been through the wringer. Even so, they survived each in his or her own way. Godfrey was a self-admitted criminal, but surely, he was first a victim. He wondered how many other lives had been disrupted or destroyed by Joseph Kony and his idiotic fanaticism and delusions? Back to reality, he mused to himself what am I going to do with them? I could just let them go. Chase them out of the park and let them find their way to Wayamba land. But Godfrey says he knows poaching, routes, crossings, and even Sudanese contacts. That could be useful. Let's test him first to see if his claims prove valid.'

Addressing Godfrey, Philippe said, "you can stay here tonight. We will give you food. Tomorrow, Godfrey you must accompany us on our scouting expedition alongside the river. We will see if you do know crossings and poacher infiltration routes. Sia and the child must stay here in camp. If you truly help us, I will help you and Sia travel to her village."

Godfrey beamed, popped to his feet, saluted again. "Sir, thank you, thank you."

To clear his head that evening just before dusk, Phillipe strolled down to the river. He gazed at the stream. It was less than thirty meters wide. Its light brown waters flowed slowly westward with a little chuckle as they moved towards the Atlantic Ocean some thousands of kilometers distant. 'I am near the headwaters of one of the world's longest rivers,' Philippe thought. He remembered that rivers like the Mbomou, the Oubangui and the Congo were the centuries old paths of transportation and communication. African migrants came this way a thousand years ago when Bantu language speakers populated the continent. Movements continued with the rise and fall of chiefdoms and kingdoms and the activities of traders and slavers; most recently the wanderings of the Lord's Resistance Army or outcasts like Godfrey and Sia. European explorers too used rivers as their guides. Henry Stanley of "Dr. Livingston, I presume" fame crossed the Congo on several epic journeys. In Stanley's 1887 race to save the beleaguered Ottoman Empire Governor Emin Pasha in Equatoria Province of Sudan on the River Nile, Stanley led his men from the Atlantic rather than the Indian Ocean. He endured great trials and tribulations coming up the Congo and Arumini Rivers, then marching overland to Lake Albert. There his emaciated team was met and saved by Emin Pasha rather than the other way around. Stanley's choice of following the Arumini, which flowed about a hundred miles south of Garamba, had confined them to the jungle for most of the route. Starved and harassed, Stanley's bloody determination kept him alive and his expedition intact. His ruthless personality earned him the nickname of "Bula Matari" – Breaker of Rocks.

Philippe's hero explorer of those olden days, however, was a fellow Frenchman, Jean Baptiste Marchand. As a schoolboy Philippe devoured literature about Marchand and his daring exploits. Marchand earned his stripes as a stalwart military officer in West Africa where he explored and fought to establish French suzerainty. He dreamt of greater glory for Mother France and conceived of a plan to link French territories on the Atlantic across the heart of Africa to the Indian Ocean. If successful, France would draw a line across the continent that would sever British imperialism from Cape to Cairo. It was a risky undertaking politically, as it might - and almost did – draw the two powerful nations into war, but it was also a precarious expedition because of the difficulty of doing it. The route was unknown and the dangers of travel in tropical Africa – malaria, food scarcity, unreliable porters, conflict with indigenous people - were daunting. Yet, Marchand persevered. He led 132 men including a company of Senegalese *tirailleurs* overland from Loango on the Atlantic Ocean to Brazzaville, then by boat up the Congo, Ubangui and Mbomou rivers. From Zemio near the present border of the Central African Republic and South Sudan, Marchand turned northward marching overland across the low-lying continental divide to the Sue and Jur rivers in Sudan. He then followed them north and eastward to the juncture with the Nile. The expedition suffered from hunger, disease, heat, overwork and hostile tribesmen. His prefabricated iron boat had to be dragged through shallows, taken apart when portaged, then reassembled; likewise, with the expedition's seventy-two dugout canoes. The journey took fourteen months, but finally in July 1889 Marchand and his beleaguered company arrived at Fashoda on the Nile, where he planted the French flag. It did not take long to be noticed. General Herbert Kitchener of the British army was in Khartoum, 400 miles downstream, where – using his army of 20,000 Anglo-Egyptian regulars - he had recently vanquished the irredentist forces of the Mahdi and re-conquered the Sudan for the British empire. Kitchener went upstream. Bedecked in full military regalia he confronted Marchand, but the two decided not to fight; rather they would let capitals react. Word of the French presence astride the Nile quickly reached London and Paris. It was a stalemate, a stand-off, but clearly British forces were superior so ultimately Marchand was ordered by Paris to give way. He did so reluctantly, but even then, driven by stubborn pride, he refused to travel down the Nile – through British territory – to Khartoum and Cairo; instead he struck out overland crossing Abyssinia (Ethiopia) to Djibouti on the Red Sea. Marchand's journey from the Atlantic to the Indian Ocean was the longest trek by a European in Africa. Marchand returned to a hero's welcome in France. Although he had not succeeded in his quest, he was viewed as the embodiment of legitimate French global ambitions.

Philippe remembered Stanley and Marchand, men driven by pride and ambition, motivated to succeed no matter what the cost in terms of human lives. He mentally compared himself to them. He certainly had no lust for fame, nor geographical or political aspirations. So, in a key fashion he was different. True, he wanted to succeed, but success for him was getting the job done well and passing the stewardship of the park he was entrusted with to others. Like the explorers, however, Philippe concluded that he did enjoy wild Africa and the challenges that each day brought. 'I hope I am doing the right thing with this LRA deserter,' he mused.

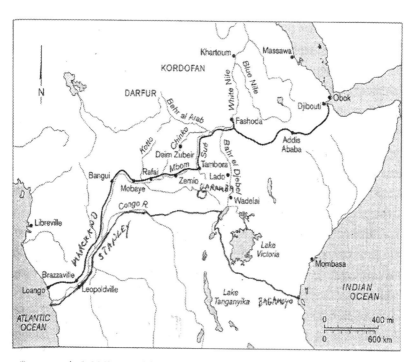

STANLEY'S (1888) AND MARCHARD'S (1898) TRAVELS ACROSS AFRICA

aking the two smaller four-by-fours, the scouting team - Philippe, Ndomazi, Elijah, Godfrey, Christopher and four rangers - left early the next morning. The track near the river was faint, but Elijah pointed the way. They had to detour back onto the forest slopes several times in order to get around steep stream washouts close to the river. Near one such stream, Godfrey indicated that LRA regulars had often crossed the big river on the shallows there and camped nearby. He pointed out where hippo trails smoothed exit paths from the river. He led them to a site that did show some evidence of human use. Ndomazi confirmed that people had indeed used the area, but not recently. Heartened by the fact that Godfrey did apparently know his stuff, the group pushed on. They paused on a bluff overlooking the river. A big Nile crocodile sunned himself on a far sandbank. A pod of hippos lazed in the pool below. They snuffled and snorted, fully aware of the men nearby. A big bull yawned widely showing off his massive incisors. Nonetheless, safe in the water he made no real aggressive moves. Philippe knew that hippos killed more people than any other animal in Africa. Their watery habitat permitted them to live in proximity with people. Hippos came out to graze during the night. If spooked by someone also wandering around at night, hippos would trample him on their rush back to water. Philippe took a mental note to organize a count of river life, especially crocodiles and hippopotamuses. It would be important additional data on park fauna.

Miles further on Godfrey said that they were approaching a regularly used crossing point. The river widened as it spilled over a series of rock ledges. Philippe decided to move up on foot. They spread out in formation as Ndomazi directed, rifles ready. Sounds of rushing water concealed any noise the team might have made. Ndomazi had them halt while he scouted ahead. He shortly returned and whispered that there was indeed a camp ahead and at least one person in it. The rangers widened their encroachment circle and moved forward. Ndomazi, Elijah and Philippe went first. They found an old man snoozing before a smoldering fire, the carcass of a small antelope hanging in the smoke. He woke abruptly when Elijah spoke. Startled by the guns in his face, he grimaced in fright. Elijah identified the team as park rangers and advised the man that he was illegally trespassing, and pointing to the smoking meat, also a poacher.

Philippe said to the old man, "I see that you are a thief. You have stolen from the park. Are you a Mohammed? You know, if a Mohammed steals, his hand is cut off. Shall we cut off your hand?"

"Aiee," the old man wailed. "Not a thief, not a Mohammed, just hungry."

"Who else is with you?"

"Just my sons."

Philippe indicated to Ndomazi to continue to keep his men hidden. They waited patiently. Before long there was a commotion. Shortly two rangers with rifles pointed at two bedraggled younger men emerged from the bush. Ndomazi beamed. "Good work," he congratulated the rangers. "I see they were armed." One of the rangers toted a short spear and a machete. "No guns?" Ndomazi queried.

"No," a ranger replied, "only these and some wire snares. These men are bush meat poachers, not elephant hunters." He laid the weapons and the snares on the ground.

"So," Philippe continued, "where are your elephant guns? Where did you hide the ivory?"

"No, no, no," one of the younger men enjoined, "we hunt only antelope for food, no elephants. Those men come in trucks from Yei or Juba. They force nearby villagers to join them on expeditions into the park, to carry tusks out. Our village is not on a road, so we are not found."

"But this is their camp?"

"Yes, we have seen them here. Crossing the river is easy there." He waved towards the stream.

"When will they come again?"

"We never know. It has been a while, so perhaps again soon."

Probably worthless information Philippe thought.

"Even so," Philippe observed, "they are indeed illegal. We could take them to Dungu for arrest and jail, but I think this first time along the river, we'll send them home with a stern warning."

Elijah wrote down their names and village. The ranger team confiscated their weapons and snares. Philippe told them that rangers now patrolled along the river regularly. If they were caught again, they would go to jail or be shot. The old man and his two sons were escorted down to the river. Philippe watched them cross. Just as they reached the far bank, Ndomazi unleashed a burst of rifle fire into the water behind them. They scurried into the trees.

Later that afternoon Godfrey showed the ranger team an elephant killing site. The bones of perhaps a dozen elephants lay scattered about. Godfrey confirmed that LRA poachers, including himself, had surrounded a herd here and killed them all. Christopher counted the skulls. "I get fourteen. All have had tusks removed, even the smaller ones." Some of the bones were covered with dried branches, other bones had been moved around, almost sorted out. Philippe knew that the elephant carcasses would have provided an unexpected feast for scavengers - vultures, hyenas, even lions, but above all insects. Eventually only bones would be left. It was nature's way. However, the covering of the bones and moving some around was the work of other elephants. It was their way of recognizing death and perhaps even mourning. An elephant would carefully lift a bone, almost like a caress, before returning it to the earth. Others might break off branches and lay them atop the skeletons.

The killing field was a sobering sight. Sadly, the facts were that dozens of other such displays of death lay within the northern reaches of the park.

The expedition returned to the former military camp for the night. Philippe planned to return to headquarters the next day, taking Elijah, Godfrey, Sia and baby with him. Ndomazi, plus the elephant census team would stay on a few more days with the Land Rover. Toma wanted to check out some areas he knew for elephants and Ndomazi wanted to better study the lay of the land for anti-poaching operations. The truck and other rangers would return to headquarters with Philippe.

In the Toyota going back Philippe took the opportunity to grill Godfrey more about the Lord's Resistance Army.

"Tell me about Kony. Did you see him often?"

"No," Godfrey answered, "he always around, but rarely with us in the camp. He have his own camps and move around much. He did visit us from time to time. We never knew when he would show up. Our commanders never know either. Suddenly, the General be there. He was spooky man. We ordered to formation or sometimes allowed to squat when he spoke. I always terrified of him. He wield absolute power over me. One stumble or critical mistaken and I be disciplined, even killed."

"What did he say when he spoke?"

"He said we did good for some raid or attack. We carried his cause. Sometimes that was all he said, other times, however, he preach about how his movement be based on ten commandments, how he was Jesus in flesh. He tell how God ordain him to save Acholi people. He say Museveni real the devil, who want elimination of Acholi people. The general speak on how Uganda lose its way and why it his duty – and ours – to drag back into righteousness. He bless a bottle of oil that we smear on our chests. The oil stop enemy bullets, so we be not hurt.

"I know ten commandments and we in Lord's Resistance Army violate every one of them. We killed, we stole, we raped, we dishonored our parents and we never know what day, so not make the Sabbath holy. Even though I worry much, I dare not talk it, even to my soldier brothers, 'less I be named traitor. We all scared each other.

"You know, General Kony he channel spirits. He talk much with them and even become them. When he did, that very, very scary. His face go blank, his eyes roll up and spit drip from mouth. His voice change because spirit take over. Usually the spirits our Acholi ancestors, but also a Chinese general who spoke foreign. Chinaman said be expert military tactics, but only order killings. He point at one of us and that man shot dead on spot. I shake to remember that.

"After spirit visit, general get silent and fall into trance. His aides cover his shoulders with blanket and lead him off."

The ex-LRA couple was not warmly greeted at headquarters, but Elijah cajoled the women into being civil, noting that Godfrey was not among those who attacked them and that Sia was, in fact, a Wayamba girl who had been kidnapped. That piqued interest because the Wayamba, although neighbors, were little known and much feared by park personnel. Philippe decided the time was ripe to make contact.

With the little family in the Toyota's back seat, Philippe had Elijah show him a track that led westward towards the Wayamba. It was slow going, eventually the track petered out entirely and Philippe was left to bash along as best he could. The difficulty of the terrain gave him a better understanding of what the American/Ugandan forces had been up against in trying to confront the LRA. Finally, they reached a stream that Elijah said was the park boundary. The other side belonged to the Wayamba. Elijah thought their village was only a few miles over the next ridge. "Well, let's drive until we cannot go further." Philippe said as he put the truck in gear and slowly forded the stream.

Up on the ridge, Sia exclaimed something. "She recognizes the valley," Godfrey stated. "This must be the right place."

Even as they paused, six tall warriors stepped out of the bush. Each man carried a menacing eight-foot-long spear and a rawhide shield. Their lean muscular chests were bare, but a string of beads hung from their necks. Skirt-like cloths wrapped around their mid-sections. "Time to palaver," Philippe noted as he killed the engine. Stepping from the vehicle, he raised his hands in a universal sign of peace and greeting. He asked Elijah to introduce him.

"This white man Philippe is director of Garamba Park." He motioned towards the park behind him. "He comes in peace to consult with Wayamba elders about how to protect these lands and also to return a child who was lost." The last comment generated discussion, then Sia stepped out of the Toyota. She said something quickly, approached one of the men and kneeled before him. He startled, then replied softly, reached out and placed his hand on her head. This man spoke to his comrades, then speaking Azande slowly told Elijah. "You may come, follow me." While several of the warriors rushed ahead, Philippe drove slowly behind the leader towards the village.

"He is my oldest brother," Sia said. "He thought at first I was a ghost, but then saw I am a person. You will meet my father, and maybe the king."

Philippe stopped the vehicle at the outskirts of the village. It was well situated on a flat area just where very narrow cliff walls, almost a canyon opened to rolling grassland beyond. A twenty-meter-wide stream flowed from the canyon providing, Philippe assumed, a regular supply of water. There were gardens. Philippe spotted maize, cassava, beans and other vegetables. Several corrals looked to be located downstream a bit. Cattle keepers, Philippe surmised with a bit of gardening tossed in. A sustainable lifestyle he concluded.

A small crowd of children gathered around the Toyota. Soon a group of women arrived in a rush. Wailing and crying in joy Sia was embraced by her mother and kin folk and swept away. "You stick with me," Philippe told Godfrey, who nodded appreciatively. The warrior leader led the three visitors to an open sided hut with stools arranged in a circle. He told them to wait there. He soon returned with three old men and introduced them as his father - also Sia's - and uncles, wise men of the village. In turn, Philippe explained who he was, who Elijah was and who Godfrey was - the husband of Sia. The men consulted quickly among themselves. Then advised they wished to deal with issues separately. First would be the park. They understood the foreign raiders were gone, chased away by the army, but those raiders had not only stolen their girls, but also many cows. How could the park rangers assure that no more stealing would be done? What about poachers who were coming back and now being more fearless in crossing into Wayamba lands to kill? The elders insisted that Wayamba did not kill elephants or other beasts, they had lived together in harmony for hundreds of years under the watchful eye of the guardian. They would continue to strive for harmony as the guardian wished.

Philippe replied with confirmation that the foreign raiders - the LRA - were gone. He noted that the thousands of Congolese people who fled for safety to camps near Dungu had returned home. The countryside had settled down. His mandate as director of the park was to halt poaching. More and better trained rangers would patrol the boundaries to ensure that poachers were located and dealt with. Philippe said he knew that rhinos no longer existed in the park; the world would not let the same fate befall elephants. Philippe said a better vehicle track would be constructed along the nearby park boundary designed to permit rangers better access. As director he would count on the Wayamba to ensure that there were no incursions into the park from their lands. He would in turn strive to see that no poachers crossed the park en route to Wayamba territory. After chewing all this over for an hour or two, the group agreed. Each side would protect its own lands and assist in the protection of the other's. Satisfied with this agreement, Philippe asked they address Godfrey's situation. Again, the elders conferred amongst themselves. They replied they had no guidance on the issue of an outlander joining the village. They would have to consult with the king and the guardian before a decision could be made. Sia and the child were welcome to stay, but the man could not. Perhaps the question could be resolved in a month's time. Philippe explained this to Godfrey in English. He was shaken by the thought of abandoning his wife and child but saw no option. It was partly what he expected. He asked Philippe to make his case. He was also a victim of the LRA. He had saved Sia and made her his wife. They had come far in order to find safety. He was willing to become Wayamba and live peacefully in the village. He would wait patiently for their decision.

On the way back to headquarters, Philippe began thinking of a plan to get a road scraper and other tractors in order to improve the park roads. If we make a very specific pitch, I think donors will bite. We don't need to purchase or own them, just rent them for the dry season.

"Elijah," Philippe asked, "what do you make of the guardian and the king references? Godfrey, did Sia ever talk about them?"

Elijah said, "most tribes around here had kings as leaders, but kings whose power was not absolute. He had to be guided by a council. Several such traditional kings still exist, but most of their power - to rule a community, regulate disputes and the like - was taken over by the government. But I am not surprised that a Wayamba king is still powerful. That tribe is isolated from the modern Congo. They still do things in their own fashion. As for the guardian, that's probably a spirit of some sort that they worship."

Godfrey added, "Sia did not talk much about such matters. As a female she fell under the jurisdiction of her father and brothers. And she was just a girl when kidnapped."

In a way, Philippe was pleased that Godfrey was not immediately adopted into the Wayamba. He intended to put him to good use on the anti-poaching effort. Back at headquarters, Ndomazi was keen to put a mobile force in the north. "I have scouted the routes and the camps. These poacher guys are sloppy; besides they have not had to be careful with no recent push back from the Congo. We can interdict them and teach them a lesson. I left a ranger there who is from the village you visited. When the poachers move, we will know."

"Agreed," Philippe responded. "Make the necessary preparations."

Philippe took advantage of the lull to canvass a portion of the western reaches of the park where the hills were more prominent. He wanted to assess elephant movements in that area and to carefully look for any signs of rhino. Because Ndomazi was engaged in ranger training, he took Christopher and Toma with him. They parked the Toyota and trudged off along a gurgling stream. Philippe asked, "Toma, have you ever seen a rhino?"

"Yes, in fact, I have. As a boy I hunted with my father and uncles, just outside the park here. We sought cob for the pot. Occasionally we would see a rhino and more often their dung piles, which males used to mark territory. Once we came on a mom and calf unexpectedly. She charged, but I was quick up a tree." Toma laughed to remember, then added, "I haven't seen a rhino or evidence of one for twenty years."

Phillipe reflected on what he knew about rhinoceroses. They are big. Males could weigh two tons. Females were not much smaller. Rhinos did not see very well but had excellent hearing and a superb sense of smell. They were surprisingly quick. A charging rhino came at a speed of thirty mph. Given its size and its formidable horn, rhinos had few enemies in the wild. Occasionally lions or a pack of hyenas would attack an older animal or attempt to separate a calf from its mother, but such events were rare.

Males and some females were solitary, but each gender

had its own turf with larger male territories overlapping smaller female spaces. Females, however, sometimes formed small groups called "crashes". Given that statistic Philippe concluded that Garmaba could have hosted several hundred rhinos in bygone days.

Sex for rhinos was often a combative event. The two involved would circle and bash at each other sometimes for hours before copulation. The resulting pregnancy would last 14-18 months. A calf would stay with its mother for three years. Given that very slow rate of increase, it would take many years for small populations to rebound.

Black rhinos were the most widespread in Africa, however, their numbers had been greatly reduced in the last fifty years due to hunting and poaching. Rhinos were butchered for their horns. Horns were made up of keratin, the same stuff as human fingernails, so have no magical properties. Despite the facts, it is widely believed in Asia that rhino horn does have medicinal benefits, including as an aphrodisiac. Rhino horns were prized in the Arab world as well, especially in Yemen, where horns became polished golden handles for ceremonial knives. These nonsensical demands pushed the price for rhino horn very high and made poaching lucrative, so much so that the very existence of rhinos was endangered. Indeed, very few rhinos, if any, are now found outside of protected areas.

Once, however, rhinos were numerous, even considered vermin. Philippe recalled that Richard Meinertzhagen an early explorer in Kenya wrote that he shot a rhino almost every day on his morning walk. East African nations recently established protected rhino sanctuaries inside national parks where black rhinos were flourishing. Southern African countries have done the same for the southern white rhino species. Alas, the northern whites were nearly extinct. Only two individuals – a mother and daughter – were known to exist. They had been zoo raised in Germany, but now resided in a sanctuary in northern Kenya.

Approaching a water hole, Philippe recognized that such places were a rhino's weakness. The animals came to drink every day and were creatures of habit. So, all poachers had to do was find a water hole displaying rhino footprints or droppings. Then, they sat and waited for their quarry to appear. The park team searched carefully around each water hole they located for prints or other evidence of rhinos but found nothing.

Over the next hill, the three spotted a herd of cape buffalo in the valley below. "Let's get close," Philippe suggested. "Christopher, you stick to me." Toma took the lead as they worked their way downhill and downwind. Philippe knew cape buffalo as one of Africa's most dangerous beasts, especially if you were tracking them on foot. A bull weighed in at 2000 pounds and cows were not too much lighter. Both genders sported a rack of lethal horns. When enraged, their attack was a combination of slashing horns and thundering beef. Toma led the team slowly into the valley, upstream but downwind from the herd, which numbered about fifty. The buffalo were not on the move but grazing around a water hole. Some lay in the shade. Red-billed Ox Peckers sat on top of several animals pecking away at ticks. Philippe always marveled at the symbiosis, the unusual partnerships, he found in the wild. He felt his heart thumping as the trackers closed the gap. Danger usually came from an animal you did not see. Philippe and Toma cast anxious glances in all directions. Christopher stayed close. In the morning heat, the animal smell of the herd became strong. Toma stopped abruptly pointing to a clump of bushes off to the right where an old bull stumbled to his feet. He was massive; one horn half broken off and one eye dripping mucus. Scaring on his shoulders and back indicated that clearly, he was a fighter. Philippe chambered a round in his Mauser. "Don't move," he ordered.

The bull glared at the intruders, shook his massive head, snorted and pawed the turf. The nearby herd took his warning and thundered off. The bull too, casting a last look, hurried off after them. It only took an instant. Soon the noise of running hoofbeats faded away. Christophe gave a long sigh. Philippe wryly commented, "well, that could have gone either way."

Later in the day the three found a family of giraffe munching away on acacia trees. Philippe was pleased to see a small calf as well as a juvenile in the group. He thought that to be good evidence that with protection, the giraffe population could expand. They crossed an elephant trail, but Toma said it was several days old and the family was probably far away. He took time to show and explain to Christopher how he could deduce when the animals might have passed; mostly through feeling droppings and analyzing their rate of decay. He would see which insects or birds were working the dung, knowing about when such activity would occur after the dung was deposited.

Looking at the trampling caused by the elephants, Philippe recalled how necessary every animal was in its niche. Elephants and other megafauna – giraffe, buffalo and hippos – ate a lot and kept the herbage and trees under control. They made and followed paths that kept passages open for all. Their defecation provided fertilizer and distributed seeds. Philippe recalled some French scientists in the Central

African Republic had studied rainfall and runoff. Statistics showed that there was more runoff in recent years, which caused silting in rivers and streams and flooding of low-lying areas, including villages and farm fields. Climate change was partially to blame on account of more intense storms, but the experts also attributed increased runoff to the decline of hoofed antelope in the catchment areas. Previously, the sharp hooves of tens of thousands of animals poked through the hard crust of the land permitting rainwater to seep into the ground. Without the animals' activity, water just ran off into the streambeds.

They returned to the Toyota just before dark. Both Philippe and Toma agreed there had been no trace of rhinos in the twenty-mile circuit they had traversed.

A week later word was received that the poachers were on the move. Philippe marshaled his troops. They only numbered a dozen. Those from headquarters joined Ndomazi plus four already in the north. The colonel briefed. "Poacher trucks arrived in the Sudanese village near the border yesterday. I snuck over and verified that indeed they are there. They were rounding up porters. I suspect they will cross into Congo in the morning. In fact, I think they will use the crossing where we caught the old man and his sons. We can be ready."

"Very good, are your men really ready for combat?"

"I think yes. They have trained well and now the test is coming. We will have solid positions and good lines of fire."

The ranger team moved into position under the cover of darkness. Philippe had night vision binoculars but saw no human movement. Just after dawn, however, a man, then several appeared on the far bank. The men, several dressed in combat fatigues and boots, carried AK-47 rifles. They were easily distinguished from the villagers who were threadbare and barefoot. I hope we don't shoot any locals Philippe muttered under his breath. He caressed his Mauser. It too was ready.

The seven poachers moved cautiously across the river guns held high. Porters carried provisions on their heads. Once in the Congo the poacher team assembled at the campground. Philippe signaled Elijah. His words blared out into the morning sky via a loudspeaker hidden in a tree. "You are illegally in Garamba Park. Drop your weapons and surrender or you will be shot."

Taken by surprise, the poachers quickly looked around. Again, the loudspeaker announced, "drop your weapons." Instead of complying one poacher loosed off a burst in the direction of the tree. Philippe took careful aim and shot him dead. Ndomazi's Weatherly barked as well, and another poacher fell. The remaining poachers sprayed the surrounding forest shooting off hundreds of rounds. The villagers went to ground. In response the rangers shot carefully picking their targets. It was quickly over. Six of the seven uniformed men lay dead. The seventh was bleeding badly from a thigh wound. One villager was dead, and two others wounded. No ranger was injured.

Ndomazi was ecstatic. "We got them. My boys did good!" Philippe was less enthusiastic. Certainly, a lesson was taught today, but how many more would be required and at what cost next time? The rangers policed up the carnage, dug graves and buried the dead. There was no other way to deal with the aftermath. They would interrogate and take the wounded man to Dungu. He would be a good first test case for the judicial system there. Elijah sent the villagers back across the river with a renewed warning never to return. He allowed them to carry their fallen comrade home. Although certain that word would circulate via 'bush telegraph' to communities all along the river, Philippe directed Elijah to visit the nearby Congolese village to ensure that the news spread.

Godfrey took it upon himself to interrogate the wounded man. No question he was South Sudanese. From a militia unit, he said, from Maradi. His team had been ordered by their commander to shoot elephants and take their tusks. He looked stunned when told his fate was probably ten years in a Congolese prison. Godfrey told Philippe that after independence South Sudan had fractured into warlord ruled enclaves run by each leading man's militia. He added that parts of that nation were truly ungoverned, that is what made it attractive to the Lords' Resistance Army. They could operate with relative impunity and outgun or out maneuver any of the local militias. Philippe reposted, "well, they are not going to operate any more in Garamba, neither the LRA nor the militias."

In his weekly radio report to Kinshasa, Philippe described the operation as a textbook interdiction of a poacher infiltration. The firefight began in response to a poacher's shooting first. Philippe indicated to Owens at the Elephant Conservation Project that he was also reporting to the minister through government channels. He said, "The minister wanted to see some positive action out here and he is getting it. I am going to try to lever it to squeeze some more rangers out of him."

odfrey continued to grill the South Sudanese captive, who spoke some English. He got names of militia superiors and descriptions of a warehouse in Maradi that was the store house for ivory. The man had also accompanied a shipment to Yei, so Godfrey got information about locations there as well.

"Well done," Philippe complimented the Ugandan. "We can pass the information on to the ministry and conservation NGOs. Perhaps they can make use of it."

They stopped by the police station in Dungu to alert the chief to the wounded poacher captive. However, the man did need medical treatment for his leg wound, so with the chief's consent they deposited him at the hospital. "I'll send a constable over to keep guard on him."

The hospital was as chaotic as Philippe remembered. There were people everywhere, even food vendors quietly plying their trade amongst the families-in-waiting as well as in the wards. When checking in the prisoner, Philippe also asked for Dr. Marie. An orderly was sent to fetch her.

She beamed as Philippe greeted her. "Hey! Good to see you again. I'm back with a wounded poacher." He indicated the grimacing Sudanese. "I have some errands to run but wondered if you might want to come out to the park for the weekend. I can show you some hippos and elephants. It will certainly be different from here."

"Sounds like an agreeable proposition," Marie responded

with a smile. "It is Friday so I can slip away for a few days. Will you bring me back on Sunday?"

"Of course."

"OK then, let's do it. Pick me up over there," she indicated a row of staff houses on the edge of the hospital compound. "It's the third one. At five?"

"Yep, see you then."

Marie sat in the front with Philippe and a ranger while the four wives who had snagged a ride to town gossiped shamelessly in the back - speculating, of course, about the patron's woman. Even though there was a crowd, Philippe and Marie had a private conversation in their native French.

"So," Philippe asked as they were riding along, "how did you end up in Africa?"

"As I told you earlier, I am from Provence, St Remy, in fact. My father was a shop keeper who sold electrical appliances and my mom was a nurse at the mental hospital – you know the one that Van Gogh was kept in. Mother came along well after him. But everyone was proud of the fact that the famous artist spent a year there and painted much of the surrounding scenery – olive trees, mountains and such. Now the hospital has even turned Van Gogh's room into a museum. Anyhow, probably because of my mother, I wanted to be a doctor. I did well enough in school and did medical training in nearby Marseilles. As part of my training I worked in a clinic that concentrated on migrants – mostly North Africans. I have always specialized in women and children. There was great need, it was almost over whelming for me a prim little small-town girl. After graduation I worked full time at the clinic for three or four years. Naturally over time I heard about *Médecins Sans Frontiers* as you know it is famous in France. I investigated job opportunities and then applied. After that off to Africa for a tour in Mali, then Haiti, then Sierra Leone and lastly the Congo. So here I am.

"I guess in a way I have a calling – my parents wonder why I'm attracted to faraway places rather than little French towns that have plenty of sick women and kids – I have no clear explanation. I just do what I have to. Life in the boonies can get pretty lonely. Sometimes I wonder what I've missed, but then I go to the hospital, save a life, welcome a healthy baby and it all falls into place. It is the little triumphs, some of which happen each day, that keep me going.

"Thanks much for the respite from the hospital," Marie stated. "It has been a hard week here. I need to get away. Besides, I have a tough decision to make." Philippe kept quiet certain that she would continue. She did, "I heard over the MSF network that a couple of cases of Ebola have appeared in North Kivu, in Beni precisely." Philippe remembered that was the little mountain town he over-nighted in on his way north from Goma. "Since I was in Sierra Leone for the 2014 pandemic," she continued, "they want to know if I will go help." Marie sighed.

"You know that Ebola was first named here in Congo. It swept out of the forest in 1976 at a Catholic Mission at Yambuku, only about two hundred miles west of here. Hundreds died. It did finally burn out, but not before being named for a nearby river. This deadly hemorrhagic fever has appeared again sporadically in Congo, but the worst outbreak by far was in West Africa, in Guinea, Sierra Leone and Liberia. Unfortunately, I was there. I volunteered to help staff the MSF quarantine and treatment center at Kailahun, Sierra Leone in July 2014.

"Experts think that the reservoir for the virus is in mammals, certainly including Africa's big fruit bats. The link is strongest for West Africa where the origin of the plague was traced back to a four-year-old boy - patient zero - he is called, who had some contact with a fruit bat. He played with it, was scratched or bitten by it, or ate it - no one knows for sure. He contracted the virus which multiplied in his body and killed him. Ebola is passed by bodily fluids - sweat, blood, vomit, feces, urine, snot and saliva - all of which are touched by caretakers when someone is sick or when they die. All of the boy's relations died. The virus adapted itself to the human body and spread like wildfire.

"No one in rural Africa was prepared for the disease. They had never seen it before and had no idea how to contain it. The learning curve was quite steep. Dozens, if not hundreds of health workers - doctors, nurses, orderlies - became infected. Most died. The malady wreaked havoc in northern Sierra Leone. Everyday life ground to a halt. In Kailahun we had an isolation camp with beds for about fifty, often with triple that to care for. The tent was completely sealed off with the infected inside. Caregivers like me had to wear protective gear that completely covered us - boots, a space suit, a helmet. It was beastly hot inside a suit. We had to pass through an air lock to enter the wards and then get sprayed with chlorine and other de-contaminants upon exit. We lived in fear of an inadvertent prick or other contact with virus infested fluids.

"It was much worse for the victims. Ebola started with a fever and bloodshot eyes - like malaria - but it progressed quickly to diarrhea, vomiting and bleeding from orifices. A simple blood test confirmed the virus. Some died quickly, others took a week or so. A few survived. Pregnant women were especially vulnerable. They miscarried or aborted the fetus and bled out. There was no cure, all we could do was try to keep them clean and hydrated, either by mouth or IV.

It was hell, we could not keep the wards clean - shit, blood, fluids of all sorts sloshed around the floor. Often, we could not even remove corpses in a timely manner.

"Additionally, medical personnel were threatened by local residents. They did not understand the deaths. White suited personnel collected friends and relatives from homes, carted them to hospitals where families were denied access, and then buried in secret. Traditional methods of caring for the sick and washing the dead were prohibited. Touching others, even shaking hands became taboo. People were terrified of foreign plots and the witchcraft being directed at them. Ambulances were attacked, health workers stoned, we foreigners were hated. Rioting occurred. Essentially, we lost trust. I found that devastating.

"Philippe, I don't want to do that again. I don't think I can do it again." She lapsed into tearful silence.

Philippe marshaled his thoughts. "Marie, surely you have done your duty, done enough. You have the right to refuse. No one could conceivably hold it against you."

"Thanks for your support and more thanks for hearing me out. It helps to talk about it. I am still pondering an answer."

Dinner that night was a decent roasted chicken and a good bottle of Bordeaux, both of which Philippe had procured in Dungu. The two talked on into the evening. Both were starved for conversation. They shared memories of home and even dissected world politics.

I n the morning after coffee, toast and cheese, Philippe walked Marie around the office complex.

"Let's go see some elephants," he suggested. They climbed into the Toyota and headed out to the nearby vantage point. Along the way Philippe spotted a few giraffes munching on treetops. "We can get closer if we walk," he stated as he looped his Mauser over his shoulder. "These giraffes are special. They belong to a sub-species called Kordofon. Over the centuries they were isolated from other giraffe populations, especially those in East Africa, by geography and by human occupation of their once vast range. So now this sub-species is only found here in Garamba, nowhere else. Their numbers are small, but with protection should expand. The problem with giraffes, elephants and other big game is that populations grow slowly. The gestation period for an elephant for example is 22 months, giraffe not as long, but the big herbivore species normally have only one offspring at a time. Lions, on the other hand, might have four or more in a litter. The key issues for re-population of threatened species are safety and time."

Philippe led Marie along the slight ridge line. Five giraffes worked the tops of the acacia trees in the valley below. Their long blue tongues encircled a tasty branch. They pulled it off and munched away, leaves, sticks, thorns and all. The beasts swayed gently as they circulated within the morning's buffet.

A youngster, who did not yet have the fifteen-foot height to reach the treetops, made do with lower branches.

By the time Philippe and Marie reached the river, the elephants, led by Old Torn Ear were already in the water. Enchanted by the spectacle Marie sat on the bluff and watched. Oblivious to prying eyes the elephants went about their ablutions. Some rolled in the mud, most sucked water into their trunks and sprayed it over their heads. Philippe refrained from talking, letting nature's sounds - the elephants' hoopla, bird songs, hippo snorts and the gurgle of water - provide the soundtrack. The crocodile was missing from the far sandbar; instead it was covered in shore birds. Most impressive was the saddlebill stork, Africa's tallest at six feet, whose bright orange knees matched his sharp pointed orange beak. His black body with a white shoulder patch gave him an air of distinction. A half dozen pelicans wandered about. Three yellow billed storks pecked in the shallows. Upstream, all on his own, a goliath heron perched picturesquely on a driftwood log.

Philippe broke the human silence whispering that they should move off. He led Marie along the bluff around the bend to where hippos crowded together in a deeper pool. They snorted and garumped. One or another would submerge for a minute or so, then burst back to the surface in a cascade of bubbles. Trails up the riverbank from the water showed how they exited to feed. There was a certain earthy stench in the area because hippos flung their feces in all directions with their tails when out of the water. "Usually they will only come out at dark, but I have seen them out sometimes on a rainy or cloudy day. Come this way, there is something worth seeing around the next bend."

They heard it before they saw. Philippe pointed to the far

bank. It was a mud bluff perhaps twenty feet high pocketed with hundreds of holes. Darting in and out were brightly colored red birds. "A colony of carmine bee eaters. I think one of Africa's most beautiful. They nest, safe from snakes and other enemies in the cliff. They eat quantities of insects, especially bees; hence their name." The whirring of wings, chirping and chattering bounced across the river.

Further along the river, the visitors came across a troop of baboons. The animals barked and rushed away. Some already on the ground, others dropped from trees. An alpha male bared his jowls replete with large canine teeth while another scurried to safety. Mothers carried infants on their backs. "Fortunately, this troop is completely wild, not at all tainted by tourists. In tourist heavy parks in Kenya, baboons learn that people have food so can be a nuisance and a danger. Did you see his big teeth? Baboons are omnivorous, but mostly eat fruit and seeds."

After several hours on safari, many more colorful birds and bush smells, the day was heating up, so the pair headed back towards the truck. Philippe stopped suddenly, sensing movement in the nearby bush. He saw a solitary elephant whose browsing they disturbed. "Quick," Philippe commanded, "behind this tree." He pointed, meanwhile he swung down his gun and chambered a round. The bull whirled, trumpeted and charged. Trunk raised and ears flapping. He came quickly bashing through the bushes. Philippe held his ground, hoping that the charge was a bluff, but the beast did not slow down or turn away. At less than fifty feet Philippe fired. With an explosion of fire and noise, the gun shot reverberated. The young bull crashed away to the right, not hit but certainly having learned a lesson. Philippe gave a sigh of relief.

"My God," was all Marie could muster.

"Yes," Philippe replied. "I'm pleased he took the warning. I would hate to have to shoot a fine young bull like that. We need him."

Back at headquarters Marie described the encounter to Christopher. She admitted she was terrified. Philippe's only comment was, "Christopher, I think that was your bull number 1, Old Torn Ear's son."

The good chemistry continued. They chatted and flirted while drinking wine and watching the sun set over the hills. Its golden glow reflected their happiness. Later that night, Marie tapped on Philippe's door. "May I join you?"

"I've been waiting."

She went to him. He held her tight. "It's been a long time, but I remember." She whispered.

"A long time for me too," he replied. "Let's remember together." They did.

The next afternoon in the Toyota driving back to Dungu Marie confirmed to Philippe that she had decided to tell MSF officials that she would not go to Beni. She would stay with her work at the hospital in Dungu where she would also prepare an Ebola isolation ward, when or if one should be needed. She added the traditional way of coping with pestilence in the Congo - smallpox or earlier unidentified hemorrhagic fevers - was isolation. A village would compel all afflicted to move into a quarantine hut. Food and water would be left regularly for the sick, but they could not leave. They were not tended. Once the conflagration burned out, survivors were readmitted to the village, but the hut and all the corpses within were burned. "I hope, Congolese remember this ancient practice. It might help avoid a Sierra Leone type catastrophe."

Philippe nodded. "I trust Ebola will not come to this region. The people have enough troubles as it is. Also," he grinned, "I am personally delighted that you will stay nearby." He gave her hand a pat.

hilippe checked over the elephant census forms that Christopher had filled out. They were neat and complete. Christopher was indeed turning out to be a gem. He and Toma were on another weeklong expedition to find and enumerate elephant herds. Word filtered down from the northern village that the killings of poachers had indeed resonated throughout the area. While he did not necessarily like the means used to achieve that objective, Philippe approved of the impact. However, he thought to himself, one battle does not win a war. There will be more confrontations and next time our adversaries will not be caught unaware. Ndomazi interrupted his musing.

"Patron," he announced, "two Wayamba warriors have arrived with a message for you."

They stood tall, straight as arrows, garbed only in a cloth wrap around their waists, their bare chests glistened in the afternoon's heat. Each man wore a necklace made of shells around his neck. The butt ends of their long spears rested on the earth. Philippe greeted the two men. Ndomazi translated, apparently, he understood enough of their dialect to get the gist of their message.

"*Mzee*, we bring you greetings from village elders. They invite you, the Ugandan and this elder (nodding at Ndomazi) to visit."

Philippe replied formally, "I thank the elders for their gracious invitation. I am honored. We three will indeed come to visit in two days' time. I thank you two for being bearers of this news. May you always travel safely." The warriors smiled appreciatively at the positive reception of their message. They looked around curiously at the park establishment but deigned to visit further. They strode back into the trees their long spears dangling casually by their sides.

Philippe watched them go. 'Men from another world,' he thought. He turned to find Godfrey standing in the office door. "Good news Godfrey. They want you to come. If they did not have a plan for you, you would not be invited. So, we'll go and find out."

Godfrey snapped to attention. "Sir, thank you sir!" His military posture hid the fact that his eyes were moist.

His war council, as he had dubbed them, convened in the large room of the rather dilapidated European style house that sat on the outskirts of Maradi. There were ten all told, most tall rangy fellows, several with tribal scarring on their faces. Commander Juma, himself a tall, thin very dark-skinned man, looked around. He knew them all well; a few were relatives, others indigenous to the area, friends from childhood. Now they joined him in his quest for power and wealth. It was a deadly game and the stakes were high. He who survived would prosper. He who succumbed would die. Juma saw life in those terms. So far, he had ridden the crest. He was the boss, the warlord, the commander. He had, through this motley collection of subordinates several hundred men at his command. He felt strong. In previous years he had cast his lot with the SPLA - Sudanese Peoples' Liberation Army. That war was long over. Former SPLA colleagues controlled the distant government in Juba, where they sucked the tits of the oil revenue pig, but they had done nothing for Western Equatoria. Maradi and surrounding regions were abandoned to their own devices. Juma was the device who succeeded. Sure, there was a governor in Yei and a modicum of bowing to Juba, but military strength in the area belonged to the warlords... and Juma stood first among his peers.

Prosperity depended on control. Control of markets, control of products - especially gold mined in the region - and control of people. Juma had proven himself particularly astute in cornering the ivory trade. He ensured that small operators sold their tusks to him and he increasingly had engaged directly via his minions in poaching activities. South Sudan offered plenty of opportunities, of which he took advantage, but the real ivory wealth lay across the border in neighboring Congo, in Garamba Park. The recent debacle there angered him immensely with a rage that could hardly be contained. None, none of his expeditionary group of twelve competent soldiers returned. When they did not return, he sent investigators who learned from the locals, those who had been conscripted as porters, that park rangers had attacked and killed all Juma's men.

Juma could not let this affront pass by. Not only was money, i.e. ivory, at stake, but more importantly reputation. A warlord could never lose. Losing was weakness and weakness was the vulnerability of a tyrant.

Juma smacked the table. The resounding blow quieted the war council. He glared and asked rhetorically, "how are we going to respond to the deaths of our soldiers in Garamba." He paused for effect, "I'll tell you how. We are going in for a big haul. Lots of ivory and" he paused again for dramatic effect, "we will kill all the rangers." His audience applauded. "Let's plan," he ordered. The group turned to the task at hand. The ten men had voluntarily cast their lot with Juma. Up to that point he produced, but several were becoming wary, sensing weakness. While outwardly they joined enthusiastically, internally skepticism arose. Juma would have to score a big victory in order to renew absolute loyalty.

Philippe, Ndomazi and Godfrey clambered into the Toyota and followed the faint track westward. It was a beautiful day. The sky blue as blue, not a cloud in sight. The temperature was moderate, scarcely 80 degrees, a light breeze wafted in from the east. Maybe clouds would build in the afternoon, but the morning was perfect. Game was not abundant, but waterbuck grazed along a small stream and a herd of buffalo rousted out of a mid-morning slumber trotted away indignantly as the vehicle approached. A lilac breasted roller sang to the passing vehicle. Near the roadside, a solitary secretary bird ate a snake, intent on its meal and seemingly oblivious to observers. Vultures circled in the distance. Perhaps indicating a kill or maybe just a nice updraft.

Wayamba warriors were waiting on the other side of the boundary stream. Philippe drove slowly as the escorts loped along ahead. At the village the three visitors were ushered again into the palaver hut and invited to sit in the inner circle. The three aged elders soon arrived. This time the senior councilor introduced himself. "My name is Lokela, I am chief of the council that advises the King. I am also the father of four strong sons, one of whom, Tomu, you met, and several daughters, the youngest of whom is Sia. On behalf of the council and the King I welcome you again to our village."

Philippe acknowledged the gracious invitation and said his team was honored to have returned.

Lokela continued, "we have two matters to discuss. First is the question of the Ugandan. Can he stay or must he leave forever? Our decision is that we offer the right to stay, but the man must become Wayamba. He must learn about our ways and be initiated into the tribe. Although never done by a man his age, if he agrees, he must join the boys in bush school where they are taught the ways of men. The boys start tomorrow and continue for a full moon. Upon completion the Ugandan will be given a Wayamba name and become fully a member of our community. He can then rejoin his wife and child."

Looking at Godfrey, Lokela asked, "do you accept these terms?"

"I do," Godfrey replied. "I pledge to honor them completely."

"Good, you may now leave us and visit Sia. This boy," he indicated an attendant, "will lead you. You may not, however, have sexual relations with your wife until you have been properly initiated."

Godfrey nodded his assent, stood and followed the young man away.

Lokela addressed the two remaining, "I am pleased that matter is resolved. It was indeed troubling, but the solution should work."

Philippe replied, "thank you for your generosity and kindness. I have grown to know Godfrey over the past weeks. I judge he will honor his pledge and be a credit to your tribe."

"Our second issue is much more complicated," Lokela confided. "First I must relate the history of the Wayamba people. It is said that our ancestors led by King Ama came into these lands many years ago, perhaps the span of life of six long-lived elders. Our people were pushed south out of lands to the north by evil men who sought to enslave them. They left behind a great brown serpent of a river never to see such a sight again. Instead here they found grassland suitable for cattle, and land blessed with many creatures and spirits. Eventually King Ama led his people to this valley. It remains a verdant place, well-watered and safe.

"One morning after arrival, King Ama went to the hilltop. He prayed to his ancestors begging their forgiveness for having left them behind. He prayed to the spirits of this beautiful place, pleading for acceptance of new people in their lands. In response a holy spirit emerged from the bushes in the form of a great rhinoceros. The two stared at each other, each taking the measure of the unknown other. Then the rhino spoke. He said 'I am the guardian of these lands. I have heard your plea for space and safety. I will grant you refuge on the condition that you, all your people and all your descendants for generations and generations to come honor and respect the land and the creatures that live on it. You must not kill or wantonly abuse the beasts, or the birds created by God. You may share the land and live in harmony on it.'

"This is how the Wayamba people came to reside in this valley. We have always tried to abide by the obligation the guardian placed upon King Ama. But that is not all, Ama and the guardian had many talks. The spirit was a prophet. Although vaguely, he saw the future. He prophesized that evil men armed with fire sticks would invade the country in search of slaves. He prophesized that pale faced men like you would come also with fire sticks to subjugate the kings. He foretold pestilence, fire, drought and flood. All these prophecies came to pass. The guardian also advised that if the Wayamba stayed true to their ways and to their commitment to honor the land, they would be safe in these lands. That too has proven accurate. We Wayamba have not gone into the wider world but have remained steadfast in our valley. Finally, the guardian prophesized that at a time of trial when the lands and creatures are in peril that help would come from strangers."

Lokela continued, "our King, who is the interpreter of the prophecies believes that you might be those strangers. That is why he summoned you here today." The other councilors nodded in affirmation. "So now," the senior man added, "we go to see the King."

Philippe and Ndomazi exchanged a telling glance. They nodded at one another and rose to follow the councilors. They were led out of the village towards the chasm. A narrow path traced alongside the stream as it tumbled over the rocks. It was slippery from spray. Light was dim as the cliff walls towered overhead. Suddenly the councilors abruptly turned, seemingly into the rocks themselves, but it was an entrance to a cave. The floor rose slightly. Light was provided by flaming torches set into brackets on the walls every twenty feet. After four torches - Philippe counted - they entered a chamber. It was obviously a throne room. Several stools sat before a raised chair. Due to poor light it was hard to see at first, but the visitors regarded a very old man seated regally. On each side stood a young warrior, their bare chests gleaming with oil, a spear and shield readily at hand.

The councilors approached the King slowly, chanting praise and bowing in obeisance as they did. He acknowledged them with a wave of a flywhisk, indicating that they should sit. Philippe and Ndomazi followed the councilors, trying to discern the proper protocol. They bowed before the king but remained standing. He gazed at them curiously, especially Philippe. Philippe was later told that the King had not seen a white man since he was young himself and never up close. He was interested to judge whether Philippe was really human.

Philippe seized the moment to inspect the throne room. It appeared to be a natural cave but had been improved by men. The floor was paved with stones, crevices or notches had been cut into the surrounding walls and each notch contained something. With an audible gasp, Philippe realized each object was a rhino horn.

The King cleared his throat. Philippe returned his attention to the proceedings. Lokela began, "the King is only allowed to speak directly to Wayamba, so I will convey his message. Colonel Ndomazi, you may translate for the director."

In a sing song voice, the King began, "the guardian has foretold that in a time of trial, strangers would arrive to help the Wayamba protect the lands and its creatures. We have been stressed by raiders who have stolen our cattle and our girls and killed many elephants. They carry mighty firesticks which are more powerful than our spears. I am told that soldiers came in noisy birds and chased some of the evil men away, but the problem of protection remains. I heard that you director and your men battled the evil ones along the northern river. I know you told my councilors that you are here to save the creatures. So, I think you may fulfill the guardian's prophecy." He paused giving Philippe and Ndomazi time to think.

The King asked, "is it so? Are you protectors of the creatures and the lands? Will you take an oath to bind yourselves to the Wayamba for this purpose?"

Philippe thought carefully before replying. "Excellency, you honor us by inviting us here to share your obligation to the land and animals. My power, as delegated to me by the new rulers of this wider country, extend only to Garamba Park, where I am fully committed to protect the land and the creatures. We will continue to fight poachers to preserve the area for years to come. Because Wayamba lands join the Park - and creatures do not know men's borders - I know we can work together...And yes, Excellency, I will take an oath to join Wayamba in this effort."

As his answer was being translated back for the King, Philippe caught a slight smile and a twinkle in the old man's eyes as the affirmation was communicated. The King nodded to the councilors. The junior man hurried out a side tunnel. He returned quickly with two more warriors leading a cob buck, a typical antelope of the region. The councilor whipped out a knife and cut the animal's throat. The warriors held it up as its blood drained into a bowl. Lokela held it towards them. "You must drink blood from the bowl, then dip your hand in it and place it over your heart. The King will do the same. This blood from one of the land's favorite creatures will seal an unbreakable oath between you and us in fulfillment of the prophecy."

It was a solemn moment as the oath was sealed. The audience was over. The King rose creakily to his feet and departed.

Lokela said, "there is one more secret for you to know. I saw you noticed the rhino horns in this chamber. Each of them, and they are thirteen in number, is from a guardian. They represent the continuity of our existence and his - and our compact with him. Now you shall meet the fourteenth." He led them back through the tunnel, this time turning left away from the village. Soon the cliff walls receded providing entrance into a steeply enclosed valley perhaps a half mile wide and one or two miles long. The vegetation replicated that found elsewhere in the area - waving grasslands studded throughout with trees. The stream trickled through the center. It was a veritable Garden of Eden. And grazing not a hundred yards distant was a large rhinoceros. "The fourteenth guardian," Lokela said quietly and pointing at four other rhinos under the shade of an acacia tree, "and his family."

Ndomazi whistled quietly under his breath. Philippe was too stunned to speak. But there they were: five northern white rhinos, the last wild ones of their species. Their only two living cousins, now confined to a protected *boma* in Kenya, were zoo born and raised. "Wow," Philippe finally stuttered. "What a revelation! May we get closer?"

"Certainly, the guardian is very calm. You may touch him if you wish."

The Garamba team approached. The rhino eyed them but made no effort to move away. Ndomazi studied the beast intently. "Philippe, he's not like any rhino I ever saw. But I saw only black rhinos. This one is bigger and, of course, not spooked and running off. However, the biggest difference is his mouth. Look, the guardian's mouth is flat designed to graze grass whereas the black's mouth is pointed with a moveable lip that lets him grasp and pull branches and twigs. So, even though both species are rhinoceroses, their diet is different." Being a tracker Ndomazi added, "their footprints are different too, the guardian's is wider and leaves a level print because he walks most of the time. The blacks are smaller, and I could tell that he was always in a hurry, by the way he pushed the ground."

Philippe reached out and placed a hand on the beast's shoulder. The skin was rough to his touch. He shuddered with the realization that this was one of the last animals on the planet of his type. What an honor and responsibility he now bore. I will dwell on that later Philippe told himself, now I should just enjoy the moment. They stood around for a good half hour watching the beasts go about their daily perambulations. The chief warrior joined them. "This is Tomu, my son, "councilor Lokela confirmed. "He is also known as the protector. He is tasked with ensuring the safety of the guardian."

Tomu said, "the guardian and his progeny have not left this sacred valley in years; chiefly because all his brothers, sisters and cousins outside were slain. We Wayamba were not skilled enough to protect them, but we have hidden and protected the guardian. It is our hope that peace can be restored so that the rhinos can again walk their own lands. I and my warriors welcome your pledge to help."

"Yes," Philippe replied, "the stakes are high, higher now than I ever thought. We think the poachers will come again soon for elephants in the north. We are preparing to fight them as necessary."

On the way back to camp, Philippe and Ndomazi reviewed what had transpired. "I understand the Wayamba determination to stay aloof from the world. Their devotion to the land is inspiring. I only hope that a great calamity can be avoided."

Ndomazi reminded him, "Philippe, the oath is binding. We are obligated to help and they, in turn, to help us. My people also oathed from time to time, especially in face of troubles - Arab slavers in our case. I understand and accept the obligations and consequences of our pledge. We must keep the secret."

The issue as Philippe saw it was the existence of the rhinos. If word of them reached the outside world, what would ensue? At minimum conservationists of all ilks would descend in order to verify the claim. The havoc caused would undoubtedly be the end of Wayamba culture and way of life. A second scenario would be the government of Congo's seizure of the rhinos; again, with disastrous consequences for the Wayamba. Thirdly, adventurers and tourists - mostly perhaps well meaning - would also descend on the region. Fourthly, and not unrealistically, poachers would know that the beasts existed. Hundreds had been killed previously for their valuable horns. The market for the product was still strong. Poachers would come again. Under any scenario, if the secret leaked, Wayamba control of the rhinos - and the very existence of both the rhinos and the Wayamba would be threatened.

Philippe was reminded of a cruising client he once had. The man was an ornithologist, a bird watcher. He chartered the boat for a bird cruise. He wanted to visit remote Caribbean islands to search for new species for his life list. Sharing his love for the quest, he told Philippe that a year or two earlier, he had been part of teams sent out to search for the Ivory Billed Woodpecker, a bird thought to be extinct in America, but of which rumors of sighting were sporadically reported. On the appointed day, watchers dispersed before dawn to designated sites in swampy lowlands of South Carolina, Arkansas, Georgia and Florida, the probable territory of the ballyhooed bird, if indeed one existed. They sat silently for the day, listening and looking for any signs of the elusive creature. "So, what did you find?" Philippe asked.

"We were and remain sworn to silence. Any evidence of the bird's existence would draw attention to the area. If we found evidence, the rush of "birders" to see for themselves would destroy the isolation the woodpecker requires for survival. So, we remain silent."

Precisely the situation of the rhinos, Philippe thought. They are doomed if the world knows about them.

ommander Juma's brother-in-law Ali was one of the wary ones. He judged that Juma's power was slipping. Should he fail to deliver on his promise to obliterate the rangers, the opportunity would be ripe for change - time for Ali to take over. He relished the idea of Juma's disgrace. He remembered the condescending treatment meted out by his brother-in-law. Good ole Ali, he'll do as he's told. Fetch this, fetch that. Always the crummy tasks, never adequate respect. Yet Ali had earned respect from his kinsmen whom he had brought into the militia. But they too were always lower on the totem pole than Juma's kinsmen. The spoils of warlordom rarely reached downward to them in sufficient fashion. Ali knew the pecking order worked that way, but he felt it was time to reverse it. It was time for him to get his due. His plotting was convoluted. If Juma's attack were to be blunted, the target must know it was coming. Under guise of planning, Ali sent loyal cousins to the Sudanese village where porters were recruited to let them know that in three weeks' time, twenty men would be required by the militia. Ali knew that this message about timing would filter across the border to villages loyal to the Congolese. He was counting on it. Meanwhile, he would ensure that his men were the rearguard for the invasion.

hilippe found plenty to occupy him in the weeks following his return from Wayambaland. There was good news from the Ministry in Kinshasa. On account of the successful interdiction of poachers, new equipment - uniforms, boots and a few radios were being dispatched. The material would be shipped within days to Bunia by air. The Park was also authorized to hire six more rangers. "Hooray," Philippe exalted. "We could not have expected more from the Ministry."

More welcome news came from Owens in Kinshasa via the weekly satellite phone chat. "Philippe, we reworked your road proposal to strengthen the rational for drivable tracks to augment the possibility that white rhinos might still roam the inaccessible regions of the park. The European Union liked that rationale and have agreed to fund the project to the tune of half a million Euros."

"I am floored," Philippe responded, "what sort of timeframe are we looking at?"

"More good news there. Apparently, an EU park roads project is winding up in the Selous Reserve, Tanzania. An engineer is immediately available to come take a look at Garamba... On that other topic, how goes the search for rhinos? Any progress? Any evidence?"

Philippe answered carefully, "so far we've found nothing in the park, but my rangers plus my expert tracker are fully aware of the possibility and are alert." To change focus, Philippe added, "better access will certainly help in our anti-poaching effort. Also, it will help confirm numbers that our elephant census is generating."

After the talk Philippe again pondered the rhino conundrum. I am gonna have to straddle this one carefully, he thought to himself.

Meeting with Christopher and Toma later in the afternoon, the two reported on their latest foray to the far northwest. "We found many elephants," Christopher said. "Almost too many to count at one time. Instead of a family group of a several dozen, the herd numbered over three hundred. There were elephants everywhere and they resented our presence. We had to keep our distance but were still bluff charged a half dozen times."

"I have seen this before," Toma added, "the large herd is a defensive mechanism. The more they are the better to fend off danger. More sentinels are on watch. Warning comes quicker and the bulk of the herd can flee."

"You're right," Philippe concurred. "Similar behavior was observed in Queen Elizabeth Park, Uganda during the Idi Amin years when that park was under enormous poaching pressure. Reportedly those big herds stayed together for years until the elephants became convinced by experience that life was peaceful again."

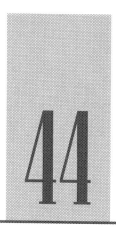

The ranger assigned to the north reported three American helicopters on the ground at the camp site. He said he had been turned away by soldiers. Philippe jumped on the news. "I'll go in person to sort it out." Taking Ndomazi along, he headed out for the four-hour drive north. They picked up the ranger at the nearby village and proceeded to the camp site. Sure enough, the route was barred by a big log guarded by two soldiers in camouflage uniforms and full combat gear. Each of them carried an automatic rifle. Exiting his vehicle, Philippe identified himself.

"Hello, I am Philippe Darman, director of Garamba Park, where you are now standing. I would like to speak to your commander to inquire about your mission in my territory."

One of the soldiers replied, "Sir, stay right here I will contact my commander." He moved off and spoke over his radio. Shortly he returned. "Okay, sir, you are cleared to advance."

Philippe climbed back into the Toyota and drove into the camp. One big helicopter sat in the adjacent field. Several men appeared to be servicing it. A soldier, also well-armed, directed the park vehicle to a parking spot. Upon descending, Philippe was greeted by a young officer. "Director, I am Captain Smith of the U.S. Army. I am the site commander for this operation. How can I help you?"

"As I identified myself earlier, I am Philippe Darman

director of Garamba Park. This is Colonel Ndomazi and Ranger Fidel. He is the one who alerted me to your presence. I know that you Americans along with Ugandans and Congolese used this space in the park previously during operations against the Lord's Resistance Army, but that was several years ago. What brings you back?"

"Let's sit down and I will tell you what I can." They moved to where several camp chairs were hastily placed in the shade. The captain asked that bottles of water be brought. "Okay," he began, "clearly you can see an Osprey aircraft over there. It is one of three that arrived here last evening. The other two are conducting a mission much further north."

Philippe interrupted, "so, this is just a staging base?"

"Exactly," Captain Smith continued, "the aircraft don't have the range from Entebbe to conduct this mission, so we needed an intermediate base for refueling. That bird," he waved at the one on the ground, "is carrying fuel. The decision was made to use this site, because we knew it was large enough to accommodate us and was far from prying eyes."

"Does the Congolese government know you are here?"

"I am not sure of the specifics, but we have a long-standing clearance to overfly Congolese airspace and use its terrain as necessary in pursuit of the Lord's Resistance Army."

Philippe queried further, "I take it then that your objective is not in the Congo, but over in the CAR or South Sudan?"

"That is correct. Furthermore, we intend to be out of here, hopefully by dark today."

"Thanks, for that confirmation. Obviously, my concern is for the park itself. Poaching by LRA personnel was a plague that we are still reeling from. They finished off the rhino population in the park and killed thousands of elephants.

Your previous military presence here in the past helped deter poaching. Especially effective was your chasing the LRA out of the area. We are trying to reestablish security in the park, but poaching encroachments continue to occur. While your aircraft discourages poachers, they also terrify the animals. I imagine that all the game in this area, especially the big guys, have fled to quieter zones. So, I am interested in future plans. Is this a one-time event, or will there be more?"

"Sir, that would be beyond my paygrade. My task is simply to secure this zone for the current mission."

A soldier hurried up and whispered in the captain's ear. He nodded, turning again to the park team. "Excuse me for a minute." He hustled off. Ten minutes later he returned. "Sir, I am advised that the mission has been completed and that our two aircraft are now airborne on the return flight. They will arrive in about two hours. My commander is on board. If you wish to wait, he would be willing to meet with you."

"Certainly, I will be pleased to meet him. In the meantime, we will do a reconnoiter along the river to check for human incursions. Okay, to leave our vehicle here?"

"No problem."

Philippe, Ndomazi and the ranger set off along the river. Once away from the camp site the peacefulness of the park engulfed them. Small birds flitted about in the riverine bush. A pied kingfisher sat motionless on a branch overhanging the water. In a flash he dived down emerging with a small fish in his orange beak. A pod of snorting yawning hippos piled upon each other in a deeper pool. Always a good sight, Philippe thought. Ndomazi spoke, "Philippe, do you remember that time in St. Floris when you took a hunter on a tourist excursion into the park?"

"You mean the time we were charged by an irate beast?"

"Yes, that's the time. I never saw you move so fast!" He laughed.

Philippe remembered; his hunter had filled his license so had nothing left to shoot but had a day to kill. Philippe suggested they visit the nearby national park that harbored thousands of hippos. At that time of year, near the end of the dry season, the rivers dried up forcing the hippos to concentrate in muddy pools. Often there were hundreds piled one upon another in a noisy smelly messy mass. These huge concentrations were unique to northern Central African Republic. It was a spectacle worth seeing. It was also sad in that the beasts, having ravaged nearby vegetation, had little left to eat. They just waited for the rains.

Unarmed, because of being in the park, Philippe, Ndomazi

and the hunter walked along the high bank watching the animals below. Suddenly startled Ndomazi leaped to one side, pulling Philippe and the hunter with him. They tumbled to the ground just as a blur of a hippo shot by them. Collecting themselves afterwards, they judged that despite the sun and heat of the day, the beast was so hungry that it went looking for food. He was probably surprised by the visitors, but they were between him and safety. His instinct took over and he headed for the water. Philippe clearly remembered the incident. It was yet another warning that men were only visitors to the animals' domain.

They continued quietly alongside the river. About twelve feet up in a nearby tree was a large bundle of sticks formed into a ball at least three feet across. Ndomazi recognized it as a hammerkop's nest. Indeed, one of the larger abodes built by a bird. This one was a real engineer. His doorway was a hole in the side. And there he or she was a dark brown stork-like bird wading in the shallows looking for minnows.

Ndomazi continually studied the ground where to his practiced eyes the story of the park was written. He perused footprints, tracks, tuffs of hair and scat. He even noted how grass or twigs had been bitten off which gave clues to who had been dining. Abruptly he motioned to a fresh print, turning to Philippe he silently mouthed, "leopard." They began to follow the trace. In the sandy ground close to the river the big cat's progress was discernible. Ndomazi lost the trail briefly when the animal crossed an inflowing stream, but he picked it up again on the other side. Philippe and the ranger followed patiently as quietly as they could. At one pause, Ndomazi pointed to animal remains lodged about ten feet up in a tree. "An old kill," he whispered, "probably by our quarry, whose territory this is." They marched on, but soon the trace turned into some very dense bush, more easily penetrated by a low-slung cat than by upright men.

"This is the end," Ndomazi announced. "Our following into this stuff," he indicated the thorn bush, "would be so noisy, we'd never find her. From the size of the track, I think female."

"Good effort," Philippe thanked the tracker. "We'd probably best turn back." Then he queried, "Ndomazi, are you sure it was a normal leopard and not a marozi, the ghostly gray spotted killer?"

Ndomazi scoffed, "Philippe, you listened too much to Mossier's campfire stories when he entertained and scared clients. Although some believe, I think the marozi is a myth."

Philippe too doubted the existence of the marozi, purportedly a hybrid between lion and leopard that turned out gray with black spots - supposedly bigger than a leopard, but smaller than a lion. Endowed with size, it reputedly had the temperament to attack humans. Mossier spun a yarn describing the beast as lean and mean, whose grayness hid it well in the dark. Mossier reported that a marozi had been troubling a nearby village; first, taking goats, then targeting herd boys. Terrified the villagers retreated into their houses each night waiting in the silence, listening for pacing outside, a low cough, and a crash through a wall or window and the wailing death knell of a friend. Mossier said the chief approached him asking that the hunter stalk and kill the beast. Mossier agreed, took his gun and mounted guard. The beast, however, was fiendishly clever, apparently noting where Mossier was stationed, and crept in from the other side to claim another victim. Mossier reported that he tracked the beast into the bush and found where it dropped the bloodied body of its prey. "I took this personal," Mossier would recite, "and returned again and again to confront and murder this evil. Finally," he noted with dramatic pause, "we came face to face. I still remembered those golden eyes gleaming at me as it crouched to attack. It came, I fired thinking I hit it, then it hit me...then, then it was gone. That was a year ago. I never found a trace of the animal, but I keep thinking it is still around and still has a score to settle." With that, Mossier would reach down collect his rifle, stand and state, "I'd best be on patrol. Good night."

Ndomazi chuckled as Philippe recalled Mossier's ghost story. "He stole that from us. The marozi is a folk tale, a monster story used to entertain and to frighten children into better behavior. If you don't, the mazori will get you. Even though there are reports of lions getting a taste for human blood, I have never heard of a leopard attack on humans. They live and hunt solitarily and just don't have the heft to go after people."

Before long, Ndomazi and the young ranger raised their heads listening intently. "The planes are coming," Ndomaazi advised. The ranger nodded his agreement. Philippe heard nothing. One of the disadvantages of age he thought, jealous that his tracker, who was older, still had acute hearing. They got back to the campground just as two huge planes circled around and began turning their motors upward so to land vertically. The park team stayed well out of the way as massive dust and debris clouds rose up from the prop wash. After the engines shut down, the waiting technicians swarmed about beginning the refueling process.

Captain Smith led two men over to greet the park team. "Sir, this is Major Wentz, my commander and Major Muhumuza of the Ugandan Defense Forces." In turn, Philippe introduced his team and they shook hands around.

Philippe began, "Welcome to Garamba Park, Democratic Republic of the Congo. I am told that you are only passing through."

Wentz answered, "yes, that is correct. Once the planes are re-fueled, we'll be gone. Sorry to have dropped in on you unexpectedly, but we have used this site previously and knew it would serve our needs."

The Ugandan added, "I don't want to impose on you, but could you please advise our Congolese military brothers of our passage. I know that a message was going from headquarters to headquarters, but your local confirmation would be helpful."

"Be glad to," Philippe responded. "Can I tell them that your mission was successful?"

Wentz thought for a moment, "I don't see why not. It went smoothly but did not achieve all the results hoped for. We had very solid information as to Kony's whereabouts in western South Sudan, our teams raided the compound, but he eluded us once again. However, we did capture his number two, General Vincent Otti, who is now handcuffed in one of the Ospreys. Ugandan authorities will hand him over to the International Criminal Court which has an arrest warrant outstanding on him. He will probably spend the rest of his life in prison."

"But no Kony?"

"Nope, he just was not there. Our prisoner says Kony is ill, but even he claims not to know where the old guy is. We've known for years that Kony rarely stays put anywhere. Still, it was disappointing not to catch him... Excuse me but I have to see to departure arrangements."

"Thanks for that update, I will be sure to advise the authorities of your passage. I would say come again but..."

Wentz interrupted, "no plans for that in the near future."

"All right then, safe travels."

The Park team watched as the soldiers scurried over to the aircraft. Engines turned over one by one and again in a huge cloud of dust and enormous noise, the aircraft lifted off into the late afternoon sky. Before long they were out of sight.

The weeks passed quickly. One morning Philippe heard a truck grinding up the hill to Park headquarters. It looked to be an army vehicle. It was big, all wheel traction and high off the ground, but it was painted in zebra stripes. "*Safari Njema*" was stenciled on the truck's door and the vehicle sported Kenyan plates. Moving out to the porch, Phillippe found Elijah already there. "Overlanders," Elijah stated, "tourists. It has been years. I wonder where these ones are from?"

"I'll be damned," Philippe retorted.

Elijah moved forward to greet the new arrivals. A dozen dust covered young people, about half men and half women, climbed down from the back of the truck. The driver and two others from the cab, one of whom said the group, coming from Nairobi, was on a traverse of Africa: destination Douala, Cameroon. He asked if there was any game to see in Garamba and where could they camp?

Elijah answered their questions and led them to an overgrown shaded area down near the river. "This is the campground," he confirmed. "It looks bad, but I will have some men come quickly to cut it back. I think the old pit toilet is still serviceable. I will send over some firewood as well." With that he went off to summon the workers as well as to get the entry- fee book. Tourists had to pay for the privilege of visiting Garamba. Meanwhile the overlanders set up tents and unpacked chairs and a table. They had pitched camp many times and knew the drill. It was nearly dark, so a game drive would wait until morning. Soon a fire was blazing.

Elijah assigned one of his veteran rangers to escort the visitors the next morning on an early game run. Even though a noisy big truck was not the best vehicle in which to sneak up on animals, its height provided good viewing. They encountered giraffe, cape buffalo, elephants at a distance and lots of birds. They stopped to admire a large python slithering across the track. In late morning, the guide spotted a pride of lions laid up under a big bush. Most of the beasts were enjoying a slumber, but one was up, sniffing and reaching into a near-by hole. The truck rolled close and killed the engine. The guide explained the hole was a wart hog hideout and maybe one or more were down in it. Soon the lioness pawing the ground gave up and joined her sisters stretched out in the shade. Cameras clicked away in the somnolent morning. After twenty minutes or so, the driver cranked the truck. It whirred feebly, then just clicked. "God damn it all," he swore. "We'll have to push her off."

The driver convinced the ranger that a shove was the only option. Thereafter the ranger loudly thunked on the truck door and encouraged the passengers to yell out. The lions got the message and trotted off. A half dozen of the passengers climbed down, prepared to push – obviously, they had done this before. One girl peered down the wart hog hole but jumped back in fright when a wart hog popped abruptly out. He dashed off, tail high like a flagpole, only to be chased by a lion coming from a different bush. The group watched as the lion tackled the wart hog not more than fifty yards away. They laughed in relief for their narrow escape. The wart hog, not them, was lunch.

Back at headquarters Philippe reckoned that if one group of overlanders had made it to Garamba, others would follow. He sat down with Elijah to come up with a plan to ensure that the campground was habitable and safe. More clean-up and repairs were surely in order.

Elijah reported to Philippe that the latest patrol from the north brought rumors of poachers. Philippe was not surprised. He knew that the recent encounter was not the last. The returning ranger said that villagers in South Sudan had been notified to provide twenty men to be porters for a poaching expedition. They were told to be ready in the middle of the month. "That's next week," Elijah observed, "and that is many porters. I suspect the poachers will be many too."

"Yes," Philippe agreed. "We'll need extra firepower. It is time I called on the army colonel in Dungu. I will go this afternoon."

With both Elijah and Ndomazi accompanying, the men left for town in early afternoon. Elijah made the introductions necessary to get them admitted into the military base just outside of Dungu. They found the colonel in his office. "Good afternoon, I am Colonel Muyembe, *Forces Armees de la Republique Democratique du Congo*, commander of the northern region. What can I do for you?" he queried.

Philippe introduced himself, Elijah, head ranger of Garamba Park, and Colonel Ndomazi, retired of the Central African Army, on special assignment to the Ministry of Wildlife and Tourism. First, Philippe described his encounter with the American/Ugandan team that transited the park. Next, Philippe detailed the Park's effort to halt poaching, stating specifically that the malefactors came illegally into Congo from South Sudan. The colonel had heard of the firefight in which most of the poachers had been killed. "Evidently," Philippe advised, "the leaders of those men intend to invade Congo again, to attack the ranger force and to kill elephants. I need more firepower in order to counter this threat." He noted, "protection of Congolese territory from South Sudanese invaders is intrinsic to the maintenance of Congolese authority over its lands. I know that is your responsibility. How can you help us?"

Colonel Muyembe listened guardedly. His expression gave no hint of his thoughts. He weighed the pros and cons. If he sent his men and they were successful, then accolades would fall upon him. But if they were defeated, he would be disgraced. If he did nothing, if he did not respond to the request, he could be deemed to be derelict to his duty. The pros had it. He cleared his throat, "yes, I can help. Let's work out the details."

The Garamba team sat down with Colonel Muyembe and his staff to elaborate a plan. He would send thirty soldiers under the command of a major to Park Headquarters early the next week. They would be lightly armed with automatic rifles, pistols, some grenades and several RPGs. Muyembe stressed that the troops would remain solely under military command, but tactics and the plan of operation would be fully coordinated with the Park team. These terms were completely acceptable.

In the Toyota going back, Philippe said, "so now, we need a detailed plan. We probably won't know exactly where or when. It will be hard to gain the element of surprise. The Sudanese will know we are waiting, and they will learn quickly enough of our augmented strength."

"Still," Ndomazi added, "we are much better situated. We will have better mobility on our side of the river and can react quickly. I suspect the poachers will use a crossing further west than the crossing where we fought last time. That would put them closer to the big herd. We can establish a camp in that section of the park and be ready."

hilippe immediately deployed two ranger scouting teams to the north. They would monitor the crossing points and, provided the old radio batteries held up, keep headquarters advised. On Monday Major Mushola arrived with the troops as promised. They decided to divide their forces for the movement north. One truck would go via the regular route, another up the faint western path. Mushola sat down with Ndomazi to go over movement details once the teams were on foot and in the bush. Mushola said that he and several of the troopers had worked with the American/Ugandan anti-LRA team in the area some years earlier so were familiar with the proposed tactics. Communications would be key. Thankfully, the Congolese radios were operative. They agreed not to attack at the river itself, but to wait until the invaders were established on Congolese soil. That way there could be no contesting the legitimacy of the operation. Philippe gave the assembled force a pep talk stressing the necessity of defending Congo from foreign invaders and sent the teams off.

Before leaving for the north, Philippe sent a message to the Ministry advising that an anti-poaching operation was underway. He also called Owens at ECP headquarters to convey the same message. He confided, "this one might be bloody." He checked his heavy gun, the Mauser. It was ready. He passed the shotgun to Christopher, who had trained with it several times. Then the two of them loaded into the Toyota and followed the trucks north.

ommander Juma arrived at the river in a foul mood. The villages where he ordered porters to be ready were empty. Not one man, woman, child or even grandmother was to be found. Outwardly Juma chalked up the emptiness to villagers' fear of being captured in the Congo, but in his heart Juma knew this stank of betrayal, but by whom? and for what purpose? He was still going through his mental list even as he was compelled to decide whether or not to continue with the poaching operation. Getting out of the truck cab, he glanced appreciatively at his men. He judged them to be tough and loyal, ready for the fight and for the reward of many tusks. "We go," Juma ordered.

The militia men assembled their burdens - weapons and other gear. Scouts were already in the river wading quickly through the shallows. They would canvass the far bank to ensure no ambush was waiting. When the all clear signal was waved, Juma's thirty men, himself leading from behind, stepped out into the thigh deep stream.

Ali and his rear guard of ten rushed to camouflage the trucks under the trees. Ali looked apprehensively as Juma's men vanished into the brush on the other side of the river. Does he know? Ali wondered to himself.

Through binoculars from a great distance upstream two park rangers watched the Sudanese militia cross the river. As Ndomazi taught, they counted the number, assessed clothing and weaponry. They also noted that a small detachment remained on the South Sudan side of the boundary. The two reported by radio. "Thirty men in army dress with automatic guns crossed at Briar Creek at 0830 this morning. They seem to be following the creek into the interior. We saw no, repeat no villagers with them. A rear guard is left on the far bank."

"So, it begins," Philippe said. "They are crossing about where we predicted. Their goal will be the big herd, probably about twenty to thirty miles away. Luckily our second army team is moving that way from the south. We will now go quickly west."

Elephant tracker Toma and a colleague were assigned to keep tabs on the big herd. They reported its location and also the fact that a three-person poaching team was also shadowing the herd, presumably that's how the invaders knew where to go.

Toma decided to disrupt the poacher scouts. He thought a straightforward attack based on the element of surprise would work. It did. That night the two rangers charged into the poachers' camp yelling and screaming. They shot and killed the three men before they knew what happened.

Among their meager gear was a radio that linked back to Juma's main force.

Upon hearing of the escapade, Philippe was shook. What if it had backfired and alerted the invaders to ranger presence? But it had not, so the Congolese side gained a slight advantage. The militia lost their forward eyes.

Juma was dismayed in the morning upon learning that the scouts had not checked in. Calls to them went unanswered. His radio tech was not too worried. He said that the radio was old and not always reliable. That calmed the commander down, but he renewed his order to his men to maintain good perimeter security as they moved forward through the bush. They pushed on.

The militia camped that night near water in a valley under a rising ridge. Juma himself walked the perimeter and set the sentries. Some of his SPLA training paid off. If an attack came during the night, he would be ready. Meanwhile a second group of scouts reported elephant evidence everywhere. The big herd was not far away over the nearby ridge. Juma salivated at the thought of dozens of bloody tusks.

Under cover of darkness, the Congolese pincher - now all afoot - moved forward. Ndomazi and Major Mushola coordinated stealthily by radio. By morning the Congolese were in position in the valley with the invaders' camp surrounded. It began innocuously. A militia sentry stood up and found a nearby bush. He lowered his trousers to squat. He caught a movement nearby and yelled in surprise. A fusillade erupted from the bushes around the camp. Juma's sentries returned fire and soon all the militia men were shooting back. Mushola ordered two rocket propelled grenades fired into the camp. The sizzle of the rocket trail and the impact of the explosion that threw dust and shrapnel everywhere added to the general confusion. The major ordered more to be ready on his command. Soon the battle took on a sharper dimension. The noise of the battle was overwhelming. Rounds of automatic fire were punctuated by the blast, thunk and explosion of RPG rounds. Cries of wounded men added to the din. Smoke drifted through the bushes. Mushola's army team crouched and crawled along the ground finding cover in the thick bush. They fired copiously at enemy positions as they pushed in closer and closer.

On Ndomazi's side Juma's militia unit held its ground. The Sudanese there were seasoned fighters who fought back. Ndomazi called for a team of rangers to back off and circle around to flank the strongest Sudanese position. Meanwhile other rangers kept shooting - one shot at a time, as their chief had so drilled into them. On cue the flankers opened fire from their new line catching the Sudanese in a partial crossfire. Emboldened Ndomazi ordered his team to slowly advance.

Philippe and Christopher stayed back behind the fighting front line. Philippe used his scope to survey the Sudanese camp looking for a commander. He saw one tall guy waving a pistol, but never could line up a shot. Philippe cradled the shotgun and watched the nearby bush. Suddenly a militiaman burst from the undergrowth charging directly at them brandishing his gun. Without thinking, Christopher leveled the shot gun and fired. The blast caught the invader chest high and sent him reeling. "Get down," Philippe ordered. The two men dropped prone. "Watch where he came from. There may be another." Christopher's heart pumped wildly as he lay there and watched the man he shot die. Philippe too knew that he had barely escaped a violent end.

The sounds of the battle resounded again with more

great thumps of RPGs. Ndomazi hollered, "forward." The Congolese/ranger teams crept onward. As the Congolese units pushed toward the encampment, a half dozen Sudanese re-grouped and began retreating up the ridge shooting as they went. They were effective in halting the Congolese advance. Their elevated position gave them a tactical advantage firing down on the Congolese.

In the midst of the small arms fire, a drum began to pound loudly. The throbbing beat was coming from the ridgeline. Cries of "Aieeya! Aieeya!" rendered the air and a dozen Wayamba warriors sprang out of the grass and rushed down the hill towards the startled Sudanese. Although only armed with spears and shields, the warriors caught the Sudanese off-guard. In close quarters their traditional weapons were superior to modern rifles. It was hand-to-hand combat, guns used as clubs against stabbing spears and long knives. Blood flowed. It was soon over.

Major Mushola and Ndomazi had their men scour the area. The dead: twenty enemy, two Congolese soldiers and one ranger were collected. Eight prisoners, three of whom were wounded, were secured. There was no sign of the man with the pistol. The prisoners acknowledged that their chief, Commander Juma, was not among the dead.

Philippe regarded the line of Wayamba warriors standing proudly by. He recognized Tomu, the leader, and went to thank him for the unexpected help. "It is part of our agreement." Tomu replied, "we saw your truck moving north and we followed."

"Yes, Yes, part of our agreement. You are very brave to confront guns." Tomu simply smiled. Philippe looked beyond the leader to the warriors. They all held spears and shields and stood regally bare chested. All but one were tall, the short one had a broad chest and a flat face. "Godfrey?" Philippe queried, "is that you?" The man snapped to attention and with a smart salute replied, "Sir, no longer Godfrey, sir. My Wayamba name is Ahtu. it means 'slow' because I cannot run like an antelope. I am one of them now."

"I see. Are you happy?"

"Very much, Sir. I have found my place. This is where I can find my peace. Thank you for your help."

Remarkable Philippe thought. He added, "please greet Sia and Amana. I trust they are happy too." Ahtu grinned in response.

Ndomazi tugged Philippe's arm. "The leader, the one they call Commander Juma has escaped. He is on foot and certainly headed back to South Sudan. I will take Toma and go after him. We will pick up his trail quickly and run him down. A larger group including soldiers would just slow us down."

"Yes, go," Philippe acceded. Capturing the boss would be good strategy and great politics. "Catch him, don't kill him." Ndomazi nodded his understanding. Signaling to Toma, the two trackers headed north.

Juma stopped running. His heart still thumped and sweat darkened his shirt. He was well away from the battle. He heard the drum pounding its rhythm but had no context for the sound. Shooting faded away and he heard no more. Juma recognized his predicament. He was alone, deep in enemy territory. His only chance was to get to the river and cross back into South Sudan. 'I have to keep moving,' he told himself, 'and go north.' He could tell the direction by the sun. The streams too he knew would flow north into the river. Although he had wanted an encounter with the rangers, it seemed there were more than rangers involved. The RPGs proved that. He still felt in his gut that he had been betrayed but did not have time to ponder upon it. He sought game trails that gave some opening through the high grass. Juma still had his pistol which he kept in his hand. He realized that even in the heat of battle, he had not yet even fired a shot.

Ndomazi and Toma also headed north. It was the logical way to go. They flitted back and forth across a wide swath of land. Finally, Ndomazi whistled. Toma joined him. The trackers studied the ground. A damp area showed a human boot print. "We'll get him now," the senior bushman stated. Off they went, now on the trail. They followed the signs - a footprint here or there, grass bent down in the direction contrary to the game path, even a lingering scent of man - knowing their quarry was near. They moved quietly but quickly. Juma was unaware of the pursuit.

The commander paused at a small stream. He got down on his knees to drink and splashed cool water into his face. When he arose, he heard a noise behind him. He turned and there stood two men. Rifles leveled. Without aiming Juma fired his pistol and heard the round smack satisfactorily into human flesh. In turn a rifle blast torn into his legs. Juma fell back into the stream. "Don't kill," Ndomazi ordered as Toma moved to kick Juma's pistol away. Ndomazi sat, blood oozed from his thigh where the bullet had struck. Dazed the tracker nonetheless bound his belt around his upper thigh and twisted tight. The blood flow slowed. "I think I will be all right," Ndomazi told Toma, "what about him?"

Commander Juma writhed in pain. "He'll live long enough to rot in a Congolese jail," Toma retorted. Toma went for help while Ndomazi sat watch on Juma.

After a long silence, Juma spoke, "my brother, I can make you a rich man. Help me to the river. I will grant whatever you wish. I have gold. I have ivory. I can give you a position of power and authority. Women or girls too. Just help," he begged.

Ndomazi was passive. His wound hurt. Somehow, he was not surprised with the man's plea. He chose his words carefully, "no, no help. I have spent my life living in harmony with the creatures of the wild. You shame them and you shame all men with your greed. I was ordered not to kill you so that you may answer publicly for your crimes. It was an order I accepted reluctantly. Otherwise you would be dead." The two men had nothing more to say to each other.

While he sat Ndomazi came to the decision that his duty in Congo was done. Undoubtedly, Juma contemplated life in a Congolese prison.

Within an hour Toma guided Philippe close with the Toyota. They loaded the wounded aboard.

It was a somber triumphal procession that emerged from the northern reaches of the Park. The Sudanese dead had been buried where they fell, but the corpses of the two Congolese soldiers and the ranger were brought home for interment. The nearby Congolese village was told of the battle and of the victory. Word soon spread across the frontier. In fact, word had reached Ali who was waiting at the crossing a day earlier when one straggler managed to find his way home. Ali quickly returned to Maradi to press his claim to the militia chief's mantle.

In consultation with Major Mushola Philippe pressed home the point that mention of Wayamba assistance during the battle was not necessary. He stressed that without acknowledging their presence more glory would fall upon the Army. Whether or not he understood Philippe's motives, Mushola liked that spin. The victory would belong solely to the Congolese Army and the rangers.

53

Two days after the northern events, the Park truck traveled into Faradje to collect about thirty members of ranger Ndobe's family. He was buried with full honors in the little cemetery at Park headquarters, joining there the seven persons murdered during the LRA attack. An uncle, a Baptist pastor led the funeral service. He preached and the congregation sang. Even though it was all in Zande, Philippe recognized one tune, 'Shall We Gather at the River,' which was a mainstay of Baptist missionary efforts throughout the region. Amid much wailing, both Philippe and Elijah praised Ndobe's bravery and service to the Congo. Similar services were held in Dungu for the two soldiers.

Colonel Muyembe took full credit for the successful operation and basked in the adulation of Kinshasa papers as a defender of the Congo. The publicity sat fine with the Minister of Wildlife and Tourism as it drew attention to his domain. The Ministry of Defense, in turn, recognized the imperative to defend national borders and decided to establish a permanent military presence along the shared northern boundary with South Sudan. Colonel Muyembe delegated this task to Major Mushola.

Commander Juma was arraigned before the magistrate in Dungu and charged with the murder of the two soldiers and the ranger. The government of South Sudan did not object.

I t took Philippe several weeks to decompress after the "battle." He was sure that more shoes would fall, perhaps upon him. Superiors at the Elephant Conservation Project in London were divided in their debate. Critics said the event proved Philippe was a violent man with no place in a peaceful conservation organization. Supporters said judge the results. The result was preservation and protection of Garamba, which is precisely ECP's objective. How can you object to success?

Oblivious to these discussions, Philippe re-established a regular schedule. He went as often as he could get away to see Marie. She was his refuge and his sounding board. He aired his fears and hopes and, in turn, heard hers. Their relationship flourished. Sometimes each of them wondered why? They seemed so different in many ways, yet they had this powerful connection - of bodies yes for each enjoyed the physical aspects of love - but beyond that an intellectual affinity. They were both on the same wavelength. Philippe thought it strange that two middle aged French people would find each other in the far reaches of Africa. Best not to mull that over, just accept it. He was very content.

Slightly limping on account of his wound, Ndomazi told Philippe, "time for me to go home."

Philippe reluctantly agreed. "Old friend, you have proved your worth again and again. I value the contribution you made to Garamba and especially your willingness to help me out."

"So now, Philippe, you are the custodian of a great secret. You are sworn and oathed. You must remain true to your obligation."

"I know," Philippe replied. "I am bound and will honor my oath. If not," he jested, "I expect you'll come after me."

"Me and the spirits," Ndomazi retorted solemnly.

Major Mushola insisted on providing Colonel Ndomazi with army transport to the border. With Colonel Muyembe's consent, he was able to reroute a weekly helicopter flight from Dungu so to deposit Ndomazi at the village across from Bangassou, CAR.

Under Philippe's tutelage Christopher and Toma spent two more months on the elephant survey. Their final count was 4,157. That was several hundred more elephants than anticipated, but a far cry from the 20,000 animals that roamed the park area a hundred years earlier. Philippe then directed the two to count hippos and giraffes. Meanwhile, he personally drafted a document detailing efforts to discover any traces or evidence of northern white rhinos in Garamba. He concluded definitively that no such beasts exist within Garamba nor had any been there for years. Philippe described the anti-poaching efforts and successes of the past several months. He added that security was not yet at the necessary level but moving in the proper direction. At some point he hoped that rhino, probably black rhino, could be re-introduced into the Park. He hoped that would put the issue to rest.

The old matriarch flapped her ears and raised her truck to sample the breeze. She sensed nothing unusual. She checked. Her sister sentinels were also alert. Behind them the herd of hundreds moved with surprising grace through the acacias. Three hundred elephants were not silent; grunts, groans, squeals, slapping of feet, ripping of branches and grass and occasional trumpeting were common sounds. The herd stayed together cemented by fear of guns and trucks. The cows watched carefully over the infants and youngsters. The bulls came and went. Although peace had reigned for some months, the elephants remembered.

Farther west the guardian shook his massive head as he gazed around his home valley. An ox pecker worked to clear his flapping ear of ticks and mites. The rhino noted a human bringing a basket. He knew that sight so ambled over to where a half dozen cabbages were deposited on the ground for his consumption. Cabbages were one of his favorites. He munched away contentedly. A youngster - one of his sons and perhaps the fifteenth guardian - muscled his way in to grab a cabbage. The guardian did not object. He had no enemies that he knew of. Nor did he know he was a well-kept secret.

The End

Acknowledgement

T hanks to my wife Connie for her forbearance and editorial advice. Her support was always encouraging. Special thanks to Debbie Jones who read, critiqued and commented on versions of the book as it evolved.

About the Author

R obert Gribbin spent fifty years in Africa as a diplomat, volunteer, and voyager. He climbed Africa's highest mountains, trudged through its wettest forests, and drove its dusty roads. He visited isolated villages, pygmy encampments, teeming refugee settlements, thronged cities, and far-flung game parks. Shot at and vilified by rebels in war zones, he experienced coup d'états, invasions, genocide, Ebola, political campaigns, and elections. He chronicled political developments and gauged the ambitions of leaders. Often embraced in African hospitality, Gribbin met people in the throes of adapting traditional values to modern times. The tapestry of the complexities of modern Africa forms the backdrop for his fiction.

Printed in the United States
By Bookmasters